"Follow me."

"We'll go and ring the rescue services for your car," Jemima told him.

"I can't see you, never mind follow you," Sam said bitterly.

Oh, dear. She reached out her hand and groped for his, coming up against a hard masculine thigh and—oops!

"What the hell are you up to?" he yelped, jumping backward.

She giggled before she could stop herself. This whole thing was in danger of deteriorating into farce. "Sorry. I was trying to find your hand to lead you to the house," she explained lamely.

She reached out again, and after a second of distrustful silence she felt his fingers contact hers.

Caroline Anderson has the mind of a butterfly. She's been a nurse, a secretary, a teacher, she once ran her own soft furnishing business, and has now settled on writing. She says, "I was looking for that elusive something. I finally realized it was variety, and now I have it in abundance. Every book brings new horizons and new friends, and in between books I have learned to be a juggler. My teacher husband, John, and I have umpteen pets, two horse-mad daughters—Sarah and Hannah—and several acres of Suffolk that nature tries to reclaim every time we turn our backs! When I'm not writing, walking the dogs or waging war on the garden, I'm often driving around Suffolk behind the wheel of an ancient seven-and-a-half-ton horse lorry. Variety is a two-edged sword!"

A Funny Thing Happened...

Caroline Anderson

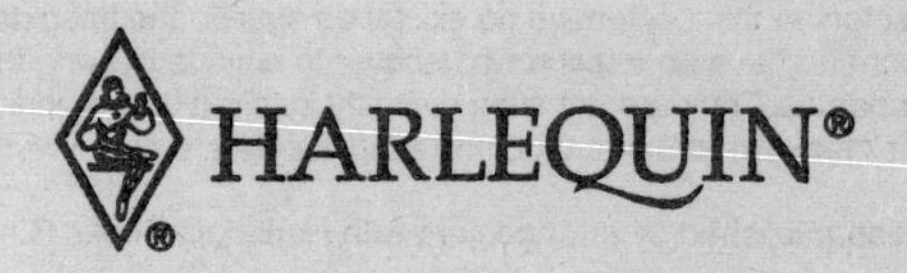

TORONTO • NEW YORK • LONDON
AMSTERDAM • PARIS • SYDNEY • HAMBURG
STOCKHOLM • ATHENS • TOKYO • MILAN • MADRID
PRAGUE • WARSAW • BUDAPEST • AUCKLAND

To Gill and Russell Darbyshire, who have been a fount of vital and not-so-vital information! Without them this book would not have been the same. Thanks, guys!

ISBN 0-373-17427-6

A FUNNY THING HAPPENED...

First North American Publication 1999.

This edition published by arrangement with Harlequin Books S.A.

Printed in U.S.A.

CHAPTER ONE

'TYPICAL! Now where do I go?'

Sam opened his window and a blast of snow worthy of the Arctic plastered itself on his face. He lifted his hand to shield his eyes, ignoring the stinging bite of the blizzard in a vain attempt to see the sign.

Useless. It was obliterated by the snow, flying horizontally and sticking itself to every available surface—including him. Still, he was pretty sure he knew the way...

He pressed a button and the window slid noiselessly back into place, shutting out the howling wind. He brushed the snow off his sweater and sighed. There was always the option of getting out of the car, of course, but just now it had about as much appeal as crawling naked through a trough of maggots.

Possibly less.

He glared balefully at the now white window. 'I thought it was supposed to snow at Christmas, not in February,' he growled, and peered through the windscreen. With the supremely effective heater on full and the wipers doing their nut, it was just about possible to see through it—to the white-out beyond.

'Brilliant,' he sighed. 'Just brilliant.'

His car radio automatically searched for local traffic information, and would override the CD player, but there was nothing, so he sat back and listened to Verdi and waited for the snow to ease. It took about half an hour, but by then it was almost dark and the howling, shrieking wind was still blowing the snow.

'Might as well give it a go,' he muttered. He eased the car forward, testing the traction control for the first time in the soft, thick snow, and to his relief it pulled slowly away. He could feel the automatic system checking the power to the wheels, giving them just enough to move and not enough to slip.

He smiled grimly. He'd bought a car with traction control because he was sick of being stuck on construction sites, but there had always been enough big blokes around to shove the car out if necessary.

Here, though—here he was totally reliant on the car's ability, and although it had passed this test, for the first time he began to have serious reservations about arriving at his grandparents' farm tonight and in one piece.

He was only able to move at a slow crawl because the snow was blowing off the field to his right and drifting onto the lane, and then suddenly the hedge on the right thickened up and he was able to put his foot down a bit.

'Progress, finally,' he muttered. He passed a farm on his left, a little cluster of brick and flint barns and red-tiled roofs next to a cottage that had seen better days. Tatty though it was, it looked welcoming, he thought. The lights were on and it looked cosy—a warm haven in this suddenly inhospitable landscape. Even the farm buildings looked cosy, with lights blazing in the barn and the yard outside.

Humanity.

He left the lights behind and was swallowed up in the eerie darkness, and he shivered, suddenly feeling very alone.

How odd. He was sick of people, sick of crowds of

sycophantic hangers-on and idiots with grandiose ideas and no common-sense. Indecisive idiots, for the most part. He hadn't been able to get out of London fast enough.

So why on earth did he feel lonely now just because there was no one about? He cast one last longing glance at the little farm in his rear-view mirror as he went round the corner.

Not a good idea.

He hit the snow drift at the end of the hedge at twenty miles an hour and came to a grinding halt, his nose inches from the steering wheel, his chest crushed by the seat belt pre-tensioner. He sat back and glared at the drift.

'Well, I suppose I should be thankful for small mercies,' he muttered. 'I could have been looking at an air-bag.'

And he had traction control. No problem. He put the car into reverse—and listened in defeat to the grinding of the wheels.

'Damn!' He thumped his hands on the steering wheel and glared at the snow. It was piled up over the bonnet, the wind even as he watched piling it higher—and on his side it was hard up against the door.

He tried again to reverse out, but it was pointless. After several fruitless attempts even Sam admitted it was pointless. Traction control or not, he was stuck.

Perhaps the farmer could give him a pull out with his tractor—or, failing that, put him up for the night in that cosy-looking farmhouse. Crazy. He was only a couple of miles from his grandparents, if that—

'Oh, damn,' he muttered again, cutting the engine and sliding across to the passenger side. It wasn't easy with his long legs to negotiate the transmission tunnel between the front seats, and he nearly did himself a permanent injury on the handbrake lever.

Swearing and muttering, he climbed out of the passenger door—straight into several inches of snow. It took all of three seconds to realise how cold and wet his feet were going to be by the time he'd walked back to the farm, but it was too late to worry. He slammed the door, opened the back door and retrieved his coat and shrugged into it.

Hell's teeth, that wind was cold.

He turned up the collar on his coat, pulled his head down as low as he could and headed towards the friendly glow of the farm. If he'd thought it looked welcoming before, it was nothing to how it looked now!

It would have been all right if the lights hadn't gone out just as he reached the farmyard...

Jemima was at the end of her tether. It was bitterly cold, her chapped and frozen hands were starting to bleed, and as if the snow wasn't bad enough Daisy the Third had mastitis again.

Some hopeful punter drove past much too quickly, and she lifted her head and listened. There was bound to be a drift at the end of the hedge—yup. She listened almost in satisfaction to the dull whump of the car hitting the snow, then sighed.

They'd want to be pulled out, of course—and that would have been fine, only the tractor was out of action.

She listened with one ear to the revving going on round the corner, while the rest of her attention was on Daisy's painfully inflamed udder.

'Poor old girl,' she murmured softly, massaging the cream into the reddened quarter. She had to hand-milk her, stripping out that quarter to relieve the tension. It was a painful business for both of them because Daisy was inclined to kick out at her saviour.

'Gratitude isn't your strong point, is it, Daisy my love?' Jemima crooned, dodging another kick. 'Steady, girl. There's a good girl. Well done.'

She straightened, pressing a hand to the small of her back and easing out the kinks.

The revving had stopped. Any minute now some townie would come tiptoeing round the corner of the barn and apologetically ask for help—

Without warning, they were plunged into total darkness.

'Damn. That's all I need.'

She waited, giving her eyes a few moments to adjust to the sudden loss of light before she went over to Bluebell and took the no-longer-sucking cluster of suction cups out from underneath her and moved them to safety. Would the power come back on? Possibly. Or possibly not.

Oh, hell. She really didn't need another power cut, especially not at milking time. She'd been talking to the electricity company about the dodgy supply for ages, but they hadn't got round to stringing her a new line.

It was that tree, of course, that was the trouble—a dead oak, hugely tall and inextricably tangled in the wires, and every time the wind got up it snapped the line. Naturally they wouldn't put in a new line until the tree was cut down. The owner of the tree was responsible, they said, and the problem was, she was the owner.

She'd asked a firm to come and quote her for cutting it down, and they'd gone away without the contract. She just didn't have hundreds of pounds to spare on something so trivial.

It didn't seem so trivial now, though, not with thirty cows to milk by hand—!

There was a noise, a crash followed by a stream of words that should have made her blush. Should have done, but didn't. She'd just used a few of them herself.

It was the car driver, of course, floundering about in the yard and setting the dogs off in a volley of frenzied barking. She took the bucket out from under Daisy, put it by the wall and opened the barn door a crack. The wind shrieked and plastered her with tiny granules of ice, and, tugging her woolly hat down further over her ears, she plunged out into the yard—full tilt into a hard and undoubtedly masculine chest.

'Ooof—'

'Sorry!'

He stepped back, rubbing his chest where she'd head-butted him and muttering under his breath. She had to lift her head to see his face, and the snow lashed against her chapped and stinging cheeks, making her eyes water.

'Can I help you?' she yelled into the wind.

He peered at her, his face just inches from hers but barely visible in the last scrap of daylight.

'I need to see the farmer—is that your father?'

Crisp, incisive, used to giving orders—and having them obeyed. Jemima smiled, and inwardly leant back and folded her arms. She loved this type.

'I'm the farmer,' she told him.

'Don't be ridiculous, you're about sixteen.'

She wasn't sure whether to be flattered or annoyed. She decided it was dark enough to let him get away with it, and anyway, she was only knee-high to a grasshopper. 'Hardly,' she said drily. 'Stuck?'

'Yes.' The word was tight and clipped, and her mouth twitched again. He obviously hated being at a disadvantage. 'I need a tow—I wonder if your father would be kind enough to pull me out with the tractor?'

She stifled the chuckle. 'I'm sure he would,' she said agreeably, 'but he's in Berkshire at his house at the moment, and anyway the tractor's broken.'

'Broken? What do you mean, broken?'

He sounded disbelieving, as if it was too much to accept that a machine might dare to be broken. She sighed. Now she was going to have to admit her stupidity. 'Just—broken,' she told him.

'Permanently?'

'Well, I can't fix it in the next ten minutes, anyway,' she snapped.

He sighed and stabbed his hands through his hair, dislodging the snow. 'Look, can we get out of this vile weather?'

'Be my guest.' They ducked into the barn, and the soft lowing of the cows brought his head up sharply.

'Are they tied up?' he asked, and there was a certain anxiety in his voice. Our city friend doesn't like cows, she thought with a smile.

'You don't need to worry,' she assured him. 'They're more worried about you than you are about them.'

'I doubt it.' A cow lowed nearby, and he stepped back hastily. There was a squelching noise, and he swore again.

'I should look where you stand,' she advised, and brought forth a volley of muttered curses.

'I should love to,' he bit back, 'but in case you hadn't noticed, it's as black as ink in here and I can't even see the end of my nose.'

Nor could Jemima any more, and she realised that the last of the light had gone. A flurry of snow followed them in on the howling wind, and she shivered.

'I'm sorry, I would help you,' she told him, her compassionate nature overriding her sense of humour at last, 'but the tractor really is out of commission at the moment and I don't have a four-wheel drive. Is it worth trying to push it?'

He snorted. 'I doubt it. It's buried up to the windscreen in a snow drift.'

'Oh, dear. Well, suppose we go and find some lamps and call the rescue people—I take it you do belong to a motoring organisation?'

'Of course,' he replied tartly. 'Not that I ever need them.'

'Of course not,' she said blithely, tongue in cheek.

'It hasn't broken down,' he growled, picking up on her dig.

'No—and of course the snow drift was totally unexpected.'

Did she imagine it, or did he grind his teeth? Too used to having his own way—and his car wouldn't dare break down, she was sure! Much too well-trained.

Unlike hers, but she couldn't afford a recovery service, so she'd taken to making short journeys and then only if absolutely necessary. 'We'll go and ring them,' she told him. 'Follow me.'

'I can't see you, never mind follow you,' he said bitterly.

Oh, dear. She reached out her hand and groped for his, coming up against a hard masculine thigh and—oops!

'What the hell are you up to?' he yelped, jumping backwards.

She giggled before she could stop herself. This whole thing was in danger of deteriorating into farce. 'Sorry. I was trying to find your hand to lead you to the house,' she explained lamely.

She reached out again, and after a second of distrustful silence she felt his fingers contact hers. They were cold, but not as cold as hers. They were also considerably softer.

'You're freezing, child,' he muttered, and his fingers squeezed hers protectively.

'I noticed, and I'm not a child. Come on.'

She tried to ignore the warmth and strength of his grip, but it was hard. It had been over a year since she'd had any male company, and she'd forgotten just how hard and strong a male grip could be. And warm. And gentle, on occasions—

'Just stay close,' she warned, and went through the barn door, sliding it shut behind her. She didn't want the snow blowing in there before she got back with a lamp to finish the milking.

It was only a few steps across the yard to the cottage gate, but she managed to smack her shin on the tow-hitch of the muckspreader and blunder into the hawthorn hedge surrounding the garden before she found it. She pulled him up the path, stamped her feet off and threw open the door. 'Come in, quick, and take your things off in here,' she yelled over the barking of the dogs in the kitchen.

He followed her, shrugging off his coat and shoes in the little lobby, and trailed her into the kitchen. A flurry of fur and lashing tongues greeted them, and she bent down and patted the dogs automatically. 'Hello, girls. Say hello nicely—'

They dodged past her and leapt at him and he backed away, crashing into something and swearing savagely.

'Jess, Noodle, get *down.* Bad dogs! Don't move, I'll

find some light,' she told him, and reached for the torch and switched it on.

He was propped up in the corner in amongst the broom handles and dangling dog leads, clutching his groin and fending off the eager dogs.

'What the hell is it with you lot that you keep attacking my genitals?' he muttered through gritted teeth, swatting at Noodle yet again. Noodle, a Bichon Frisé and first cousin of the floor-mop he was leaning on, leapt up his leg again, grinning eagerly, the silky cords of her wild off-white coat falling around her like tangled spaghetti.

'I'm sorry.' She stifled a laugh and slapped her thigh. 'Noodle, come here, sweetheart. Stop it.' The dog came, quite unrepentant, and her guest straightened and looked at her. She couldn't quite read his expression, so she shone the torch full in his face and he ducked his head, flinging his arm up to cover his eyes.

'What the hell are you trying to do now—blind me?' he snapped.

'Sorry,' she said again, but she wasn't. In that split second before she'd lowered the torch she'd seen enough to make her pulse do stupid and erratic things. His eyes were startling—dark blue, almost navy, stunning against the winter white of his skin and the dark slash of his brows, and just now they were spitting sparks. His hair was thick, upended by the wind so that he looked rumpled and sexy and gorgeous, and that mouth, if it wasn't snarling—

She swung the torch round and hunted for the lantern and matches, then fiddled for ages trying to light it while he stood waiting in the shabby kitchen, frustration coming off him in tangible waves.

Thank God it was dark, she thought. Maybe by lamplight the tired room would look cosy and romantic—and maybe she'd look a bit more presentable and less as if she'd been tumbled in the haybarn, but it was unlikely. She finally got the wick to burn, and trimmed it and put the glass globe back. The flame spluttered and steadied, and she held it up and looked up at him—and up, and up…

'You're tiny,' he said accusingly, as if it were a fault in her that she should have tried to overcome.

'Sorry, but the best things come in little packages,' she quipped, and tried to ignore the race of her pulse. 'Now, why don't you go in the parlour and ring the rescue people before it's so bad they won't come out?'

She handed him the lantern and pushed him towards the parlour door. 'Phone's in there.'

'Where am I? I need to tell them how to get here.'

She met his eyes and knew this was going to be embarrassing. It had seemed fun at the time when she'd changed the name, but now—

'Puddleduck Farm,' she told him, and felt her chin rise challengingly.

'Pu—right,' he said, letting out his breath. Humour danced in his midnight eyes, but to his credit he kept it in—to a point. Then he blew it. 'Don't tell me—your name's Jemima.'

She breathed in and drew herself up to her full five feet nothing. 'That's right,' she told him, and dared him to comment.

His mouth twitched but he said not another word. 'Nice to meet you, Jemima,' he said with a courtly, mocking little bow. 'Samuel Bradley. At your service.'

'I thought I was at yours,' she said drily.

His mouth twisted in a wry smile, and her heart did

a crazy hiccup. 'You are—and I'm very grateful. I'll ring them.'

She left him to it and went back into the kitchen, filling the kettle and standing it on the hob by torchlight. She could hear his voice rising, but she guessed it was fruitless. Against the window she could see the swirling snow, bright in the torchlight, falling now in great fat flakes that would cut them off without doubt. She threw the dirty crockery into the sink and ran hot water over it, trying to hide it.

Hopeless. She needed to spend hours in here, but there just wasn't the time in the day, and by the evening she was bushed—

He stomped into the kitchen, a look of disgust on his face, and set the lantern down with a little smack. The flame flickered and steadied.

'Problems?' she said mildly. She knew there would be.

'They can't come,' he growled. 'They're flooded with calls and they can't do anything until tomorrow.' He glanced at his watch, a thin flat disc of gold on a plain leather strap, simple and tasteful—and why was she even noticing?

'Mind if I ring the people I'm going to? They'll be expecting me and I don't want them to worry.'

'Of course. Be my guest. You can stay the night, if you like.'

'Oh, that won't be necessary. I'm sure I can walk to them from here; it can't be far.'

'In this?' She shone the torch at the window again and he swore. He was doing that rather a lot. Obviously a man who liked things his own way. He'd better not take up farming, then, she thought with an inward sigh. She'd got thirty cows out there to milk without power, not to mention the calves to feed and water to fetch and eggs to collect, and it was going to be hell—starting shortly.

'I'll ring them,' he muttered, and went back into the parlour with the lantern.

'Hi, Gramps, it's Sam. Look, I've had a minor hiccup. I've got the car stuck in a drift at Puddleduck Farm. How far is that from you? Can I walk?'

'Puddleduck? Oh, that's only—'

'Puddleduck?' his grandmother said in the background. 'Give that to me. Hello, Sam?'

'Hello, Grannie. I was just telling Gramps I'm at Puddleduck Farm. The car's stuck in a drift, so I was going to walk—'

'Oh, no, not in this! It's much too far! You stay there, Jemima will look after you—'

'You know her?'

'Oh, yes, we're neighbours—well, sort of,' she rushed on. 'It's quite a distance, though, a good two miles, and in this snow and the dark—no, darling, it's not safe; you stay there with Jemima. Perhaps you can give her a hand—she's on her own and with the power out she'll have to milk by hand—she could probably use your muscles to help with the other chores.'

He heard his grandfather snort in the background, and could have groaned aloud. Help her—in this? He hated the cold, and most particularly he hated cows. He looked down at his socks and trousers, covered at the ankle with a malodorous plastering of dark green, courtesy of one of the aforementioned, and sighed. He could just see the look he'd get at the dry cleaners!

'I'm sure she can cope—'

'Oh, Sam! She's on her own and she's a tiny slip of a thing. You can't abandon her!'

He crumbled. 'OK, Grannie,' he surrendered. He knew when he was beaten, and if there was one thing his grandmother had always been able to do, it was to sort out his priorities. That, after all, was why he was coming to see her now.

'Will you be all right?' he asked belatedly.

'Oh, yes. We've got a lovely warm house, and lots of wood inside the porch. We'll be fine—after all, we've got no animals to worry about now apart from the dogs and cats. We'll just wait it out. You just look after Jemima, and keep in touch. Give her our love.'

He said goodbye and cradled the phone thoughtfully. Look after Jemima, eh? From the brief glimpse he'd had of her that wouldn't be necessary—she seemed more than capable of looking after herself, tiny though she might be. He went back into the kitchen and set the lamp down, just as she poured the tea.

'All right?' she asked brightly, and turned round.

The lamplight caught her eyes, golden brown and mellow with a hint of mischief, matching the smile on her chapped lips and the chaotic tumble of curls that rioted around her head. She looked young and vulnerable and incredibly lovely, and he had a sudden shaft of suspicion about his grandmother's motives.

'My grandparents send their love,' he said, watching her closely. 'Dick and Mary King.'

Her eyes widened. 'You're their grandson?'

'Yes. I was on my way to stay with them, only it's apparently too far to walk, my grandmother said. She suggested I should stay here and help you—if you really did mean it when you offered me a bed for the night?'

* * *

Jemima looked hard, but she couldn't see a thing where his halo ought to be. It must be on Mary's head, she thought, and stifled a smile. It was barely three hundred yards over the fields to Dick and Mary's little farmhouse, and Mary knew it. So would Sam, when he realised where he was, and who she was.

Help her, eh?

She eyed her captive farmhand with interest. Six foot, at least, and well muscled under the sweater. He'd grown up nicely...

Yes, he'd do. A bit soft, of course, but he was proud enough to work through that. All she had to do was appeal to his ego.

Bless Mary. What a regular sweetheart!

'Thanks—that would be great,' she agreed, and smiled the first genuine smile since he'd arrived.

'I'll pay you for the accommodation, of course,' he said quickly—doing things correctly again, of course. Her smile widened.

'That's OK—I'll take payment in kind.' She ran her eyes over his body, openly assessing him, and to her delight he coloured. He really hadn't changed much at all. 'You look fairly useful,' she went on, a smile teasing round her lips. 'Have you got stamina?'

'I'm sure I can keep up with you,' he said blandly, recovering his composure. His lips twitched, and her eyes were drawn to the fine sculpted lines of his mouth. Not too full, but not skimpy, either. She'd lay odds he'd learned to kiss—

'I'd better find you something to wear—unless you've got anything you want to get from the car?' she said hastily, backing off from this banter before she talked herself into more trouble than she could handle. After all, they were trapped alone together. Just because he'd been a nice boy didn't mean he was a reliable adult. He could be a serial killer, or a rapist—! 'Perhaps some jeans?'

'I've got some—thank God. I can just see me squeezed into a pair of your tiny little jeans. Yet another assault on the family jewels,' he said drily.

She blushed, ignoring his remark, or at least the last part of it. 'I was going to offer you something of my uncle's, but if you've got things in the car we might as well get them before it gets worse.'

He looked at the snow swirling up against the window and his face was a picture. He obviously didn't relish going out in it any more than she did, but the difference was she had to and he didn't.

She had a sudden pang of conscience, and stifled it. He was big enough and ugly enough to look after himself, she decided, and anyway, they were his clothes. Whether he would help with the cows had yet to be seen.

'Well?'

'I wonder if it might make more sense to do it in the morning?'

'You might not find the car in the morning,' she pointed out in fairness, and then added, 'I don't suppose you thought to tie anything on the aerial?'

'Like what?' he said wryly. 'Party balloons? Anyway, it doesn't have an aerial.'

'Oh.' Funny, with those expensive-looking clothes she would have thought he could have afforded a car with a radio, but whatever. 'We ought to mark it with something red, so a snow plough doesn't come along and upend it into the hedge. It's been done before.'

He went pale, poor love. 'Oh,' he said tightly. 'I haven't marked it. Do you have anything red?'

She thought, and the only thing that came to mind

was a bra—a lacy confection that she didn't wear any longer. After all the cows didn't give a tinker's cuss if she wore sexy undies, and frankly the plain cotton crop-top style bras were more comfortable when she was working.

Still, she wasn't sure she was ready to let him tie it to his car!

'Maybe,' she conceded. 'I'll have to look. We'll tie it to a stick and shove it in the drift. If it's attached to the car it might get covered.'

'Covered?' he exclaimed.

She shrugged. 'Whatever, we need to get your gear out. I think there might still be a pair of boots here your sort of size—here, try these.'

She turned them upside down and banged them, and a huge spider fell out and ran across the floor.

'What the hell was that?' he yelled, backing up into the kitchen. The collie chased the spider and cornered it, then barked at it.

'Just a spider—Jess, stop it! You're daft. Here, try them on.'

He took the boots suspiciously. 'Any cousins down there?' he asked, peering down the tops.

'Possibly. Tuck your trousers into your socks, just in case. Is that the best coat you've got?'

He pushed his feet into the wellies with a shudder and stood up. 'Yes. Why?'

'Because apart from the fact that it'll get filthy, it's not waterproof, and when the snow melts on you, you'll get soaked and freeze.'

'I can hardly wait,' he muttered.

Jemima took pity on him and banged out an old waxed jacket, checking the sleeves for spiders before handing it over. 'Here, try this.'

He pulled it on and looked instantly more like a farmer and less like a townie. Amazing what the right uniform could do to a man. He almost looked as if he could cope with a cow—except for the fine wool trousers that were going to get hopelessly ruined unless he changed.

'What about the red thing to tie to a stick?'

'Ah.' She ran upstairs, found the red bra and a matching suspender belt, and stuffed them into a pocket. She'd tie them on when he wasn't looking…

'Let's go and get your gear,' she said, arriving back in the kitchen and pulling on her own coat and boots. She told the dogs to stay and headed out into the blizzard, torch in hand. She picked up a couple of stakes from the corner by the shed, and headed across the yard towards the lane.

He followed her, not more than a few inches away all the way to the car, and so she heard his muttered exclamation when they found it almost totally buried under the snow drift.

'Where's the case?' she asked.

'In the boot.' He eyed the smothered boot with jaundice. 'I suppose I'd better brush the snow off first.'

'Probably,' she agreed, and held the torch while he swiped at the light powdery heaps. It reminded her of why you couldn't make a decent sandcastle with dry sand—it just kept on pouring down. In the end he swore in exasperation and just opened the boot, hauled out a smart garment bag and a monogrammed leather sports bag, and slammed the lid before the entire snow drift slid inside.

And so much for him not being able to afford a car with a radio, she thought, eyeing the BMW logo on the boot lid with jaundice. It probably had a gadget to pick up radio waves by telepathy!

'I'd better lock it,' he muttered, pointing the remote control at the car, and Jemima stifled a laugh. City types, she thought, and tried to forget that until just under a year ago she'd been one too.

'I'll put these sticks up,' she told him, and, rummaging in her pocket, she pulled out the underwear, tied it to the sticks and then took one to the front, ramming it in by the side of the bumper where it would stay up and show.

She struggled back past the car, grabbed the other stick and was pushing it into place when Sam took the torch from her hand and pointed it at her 'flags'.

'What the—?'

'Don't you dare laugh,' she warned him, but it was too much.

A chuckle rose in his throat, and without thinking she scooped up a handful of snow and shoved it down his miserable neck.

He let out a yell that would have woken the dead and returned the favour, and a huge glob of snow slid down her front and lodged in her bra.

'Touché!' she said with a laugh, and backed off, pulling her clothes away from her chest and shaking the snow out.

'Pax?' he asked warily, hefting a fresh snowball just in case.

She considered revenge, and then decided she'd get her own back on him in the next few hours anyway—in spades!

'Absolutely,' she agreed. 'I'm cold enough without snow in my underwear. You can drop that.'

'Not yet—just look on it as insurance,' he told her,

and she flashed the torch at him and caught a lingering smile that transformed his face and did odd things to her insides.

They headed back down the lane, bent over to shelter from the driving blizzard, and made it back to the cottage without incident.

'I should change into jeans,' she advised as they shed their outer gear and went back into the lamp-lit kitchen. 'It can get mucky in the barn.'

'Mucky?' he said with suspicion, and she smiled.

'That's the one,' she said cheerfully. 'I should change in here—I'll go and dig out some sheets and make up your bed while you do that.'

She pulled off her hat, shook the snow off her hair and ran upstairs with the torch, her socks soundless on the threadbare carpet. She decided to put him in the room over the parlour. After hers, which was over the kitchen, it was the warmest.

It was also right beside hers, which might not be such a good move. She eyed the doors of the other rooms, but they were small, cold and full of boxes that she still had to sort out.

She'd have to put up with his proximity, and not get into any more playful snowball fights with him that might lead on to other things. She was finished with all of that. She didn't need it—or rangy, sexy men with wicked smiles and attitude. She made the bed up and tried not to think about what he was doing downstairs with those incredible long legs of his.

She tugged the quilt straight, patted the pillows and went back down, taking the torch with her. Again, her socks made no sound, and she arrived in the kitchen to find him crouched down in his designer jeans, scratching the dogs behind their ears.

Amazing.

'I should watch Jess, she doesn't like men much,' she warned.

'Jess?'

The collie pricked her ears and looked longingly at him.

'Short for Jezebel,' she muttered. Faithless mutt. Apart from Sam's grandfather she'd bitten every other man who'd crossed the threshold since Uncle Tom had died!

'Come on, let's go and get this milking started. The sooner we start, the sooner we'll finish. Ever milked a cow before?'

He shuddered. Not a good sign. 'No, thank God.'

'Oh. Oh, well, you'll learn, I suppose. I wonder how long this power cut will last?'

'Phone the electricity board. They usually have an idea.'

Stupid. She should have thought of that. If she hadn't been so distracted by him, she probably would have done it ages ago. She took the torch into the parlour and rang up. It did nothing for her mood.

'Unknown fault,' she told him disgustedly. 'Could be hours—it sounds like a huge area's out. I thought it was my tree.'

'Shorting out the whole of Dorset? It must be a hell of a tree.'

She laughed. 'In its day, maybe. Now it's just a pain. Come on, let's turn you into a country boy. Ever seen the film *City Slickers*?'

He gave her a dirty look. She deserved it. It was a cheap shot.

'Come on, townie,' she said more kindly. 'Let's see

what you're made of. I'm sure I can find you something safe to do.'

She grabbed her coat, shoved her feet into her boots and picked up the lantern. 'OK, cowpoke. Let's be having you.'

He met her eyes without a word, and she saw him pick up her challenge like a gauntlet. Oh, lawks. She was in way over her head.

She tugged her hat down hard and went out into the blizzard...

CHAPTER TWO

HER revenge for the snowball came sooner than she expected. It took Daisy ten seconds to check Sam out and decide he needed butting in the ribs, and he leapt backwards with a grunt and smacked into the wall.

'Daisy, that's not nice,' Jemima chided, and turned her attention to her crippled farmhand. 'Are you OK?' she asked, eyeing his pinched mouth and closed eyes with concern. After all, it would be such a waste of all that God-sent muscle if he was really injured—

'Oh, I'm fine, just peachy,' he wheezed, and his eyes flickered open and speared her. 'Can't you—tie her up, or something? In fact, can't you tie them all up?'

'I don't need to. It's milking time. If I feed them they'll go and stand in their stalls ready.'

'Well, feed them then, for heaven's sake!' he pleaded, and levered himself off the wall, feeling his ribs cautiously.

Jemima gave a little shrug and grabbed a pitchfork, then started forking silage into the trough in front of each cow. They knew the routine, and lined up patiently waiting as she worked her way down each side of the barn.

'Can I do that for you?' he offered, eyeing her safe position on the other side of the barrier.

He certainly could. She handed him the fork, took another one and cleared away the straw under each animal's udder, ready for milking. Now all she needed was the hot water. She handed Sam a bucket.

'Could you go into the house and bring some hot water, please? Not too hot—it's to wash their udders.'

His eyes widened, but he took the bucket and the torch and headed for the door. 'I am going out—I may be some time,' he murmured theatrically, and then the door opened and the Arctic screamed in on a frigid blast. He ducked his head, shot out and slid the door back into place, shutting out the blizzard.

Jemima grinned and set up the milking stool and bucket, then looked round the barn and lost her smile. She'd have to muck out in the morning, so she hoped the power would be back on because milking by hand took so long she'd be hardly finished before she had to start again, and she didn't think for a moment that her intrepid explorer was going to make much of a milkman.

He reappeared, hair on end again, a steaming bucket in his hand and Jess by his side. 'She was desperate to come—is that all right?'

'Sure.' She smiled and held out her hand, and Jess came running up for a quick pat before finding a cosy corner and flopping down, one watchful eye open. Jemima took the bucket and the old flannel she used to wash them, and started on the first udder.

Normally she'd connect them up to the old Fulwood milking plant Uncle Tom had bought in 1949 and never got round to changing, but without power she had no option but to crouch on the little stool by each cow in turn, and strip the milk out of all four quarters by hand. It was a slow process, and she could see Sam was bored, so she cocked her head round towards him and grinned.

'So, what do you usually do for entertainment on a Friday night?'

He laughed and hunkered down beside her, watching.

'Oh, this and that. Murder a few grannies, rob the odd bank—nothing special.'

'There's a picture of you in the police station—or was that Buffalo Bill?'

'Probably—we're very alike,' he said, absolutely deadpan.

'Mmm—except he can milk cows, of course.'

A brow arched—just ever so slightly—and she wouldn't have noticed if she hadn't been taking such a close interest in his features. However, she had noticed. Was it a challenge? She wasn't sure, but she stood up anyway and gave him the stool.

'Come on, Buffalo Bill, your turn.'

He folded himself up onto the stool and gave her a steady look that spoke volumes. Her estimation of him went up a notch, and she folded her arms and propped herself on Bluebell's nicely rounded rump.

He reached for the udder tentatively, and Bluebell turned her large, gentle head and eyed him in surprise. It was odd enough being milked by hand, something that happened very rarely, but this stiff, taut man—well!

'Rest your head on her flank,' Jemima instructed, and he gave her an old-fashioned look.

'Rest my head?' he said, as if she'd suggested he should put it in a lion's mouth. She stifled a laugh.

'Yes—you know, lean on her.'

He arched an eyebrow disbelievingly, and allowed his head to touch her side. 'Now what?'

'Pull the teat down, and then close your fingers from the top down to the bottom, as if you're squeezing the milk out like toothpaste—that's it!'

A little squirt of milk shot out of the teat and splashed on his jeans.

'Now try and get it in the bucket.'

He gave her a dirty look, shook his head despairingly and carried on. He was doing really quite well until Bluebell moved and knocked the bucket over.

'Hell!'

He leapt to his feet, ducking out of the way of the flying milk and startling Bluebell, who shot across the barn towards Jemima, rolling her eyes and snorting softly.

'It's all right, sweetheart, he's just a city boy,' she crooned comfortingly, squashing her laughter. 'Come on, my love.'

'Come on my love, nothing,' he muttered, watching her balefully as she led the anxious cow back across the barn to her stall and gave her more silage. 'Why did she do that?'

'I expect you tickled her—they're very sensitive.'

'Sensitive!' he exclaimed. 'They're a bunch of loonies!'

'Just ignore him, darlings,' she told the cows. 'He's only a man; he can't be expected to understand.'

One of them lowed at her, a warm, soft sound of agreement, and Sam snorted in disgust. Smiling, Jemima went back to her place beside Bluebell, quickly finished off and moved on to the next cow.

'Why do you wash the udders?' he asked, following her but standing safely out of range. 'They don't look dirty.'

'To clean them, of course, just in case, but also because it helps the let-down.'

'Let-down?'

She smiled into Ruby's side. 'They have to give you the milk. If it was just a tank it would run out. You have to persuade the udder to relax—'

'Right.'

He didn't sound convinced. Ruby understood the system, though, and was easy to milk, but then she'd had mastitis quite recently and had had to be hand-milked for some time. There were others who were much harder to do.

'What happens to the milk once you collect it?'

'It gets filtered and poured into the cooling tank—oh, no!'

'What?'

'No power! The cooler won't be working, and the paddles won't be stirring, so the milk will separate and go off—not that they'll be able to collect it anyway...'

'And?'

'And so I won't get paid for it, and I'll lose money.'

'Much?'

She thought of the useless tractor, the state of her car and the even more precarious state of her bank balance.

'More than enough,' she said grimly.

'Is there anything you can do about that?'

She straightened up, looking at the placid cows waiting patiently for her attention. It would take for ever to milk them all, and it would all have to go down the drain—

'I need to put the fresh calvers back with their calves. That will feed the calves, stop me having to milk their mums until the power's back on and save the wasted milk until the tanker can get through again.'

'How many are fresh calvers?'

She sighed. 'Only ten.'

'So you've got—what, twenty more?'

She nodded. 'Yes. Twenty-one, in fact. We ought to sort them out now; they're getting uncomfortable because I'm late.'

It was another half-hour before the fresh calvers and

their offspring were reunited, and then the others needed milking urgently. Jemima looked into the water trough and sighed. Already it was almost empty—

'What is it?'

'The water trough. It needs filling up—the well water pump is electric.'

'Wouldn't you know it?' he muttered. 'Where's the nearest tap?'

'The water in the house is electrically pumped. We don't have mains.'

'What!'

'The water's beautiful—it comes from deep aquifers and the taste is so clear, so pure, you—you just wouldn't believe it.'

'But mains is so easy.'

She shook her head. 'The milk wouldn't taste the same, and I sell it to a specialist firm—they make clotted cream and yoghurt with it. The quality of the milk is everything.'

He sighed. 'What are you telling me?'

'The water has to come from the stream. There's a little step to stand on while you dip the buckets. I'll show you.'

'I can hardly wait,' he muttered under his breath, but he came with her, saw the stream, hung up a lantern between the barn and the stream and started bucketing the water while she milked.

'How many do I need to bring?' he asked after the tenth trip or so.

She looked up and took pity on him. He was propped against the wall, breathing hard, and he'd hardly started.

'About a hundred and fifty buckets,' she told him.

His eyes widened. 'How—? A hun—! That's ridiculous,' he said flatly.

'They drink about ten to fifteen gallons a day. That's at least three hundred gallons, or a hundred and fifty buckets. It's only seventy-five trips a day.' She relented at his look of horror. 'It won't need that many tonight, and I expect the power will be back on by the morning.'

He shouldered away from the wall without another word, and went back out. The wind was still howling, she noticed, and although it had stopped snowing there was a fine stinging spray of snow being carried off the field and straight into his face as he came back to the barn.

She finished the last cow, poured the milk into the cooler just in case the tanker was able to get through tomorrow by a miracle and the power came back on soon, and then went to help him.

They finished the water at ten o'clock. By that time her hands were bleeding freely from the many cracks in her fingers, her palms were raw, her back was screaming and if she'd been on her own she would have curled up and wept.

She wasn't, though, so she didn't.

Nor did Sam, and, casting him a quick look, she thought that left alone he'd probably want to do the same!

'You'll be stiff in the morning,' she warned.

'Tell me about it. Anything else to do tonight?'

'Only eat, if I can find anything worth cooking.'

'Shall I nip out for a Chinese?'

She met his eyes, and was amazed to see humour lurking there still, after all they'd done. All *he'd* done, and him just a city boy.

'Good idea. I'll have special chow mein.'

'OK. I'll have rice and lemon chicken—fancy a spring roll?'

She looked round the barn one last time, took the lantern down and glanced at him. 'Oh, yes—and prawn crackers.'

His stomach rumbled loudly, and she gave a quiet, weary laugh. 'Come on, cowboy, let's go and raid the larder.'

Sam was dog-tired. He didn't remember ever being so tired in his life, but he supposed it was possible. His hands hurt from carrying so many buckets, his back and shoulders ached with the unaccustomed exercise and he was so hungry he had the shakes.

'Anything I can do?' he offered, hoping to speed things along.

'No—there's some bread and cheese and there's some soup left in the fridge—I'll heat it up. Wash your hands, but be frugal with the water, the tank won't refill—in fact, use my water, here.'

She shook her hands off and picked up the towel, and he went over to the sink and looked down into the bowl of water. The bar of soap was streaked with red, and he looked over his shoulder and watched as she pressed the towel against her fingers cautiously and winced.

He scrubbed his hands clean, wiped them on the towel and then went over to her, taking the cheese from her and putting it down, then lifting her hands in his and turning them over.

They were cracked and ingrained with dirt, the skin rough and broken although it had stopped bleeding, and she stood there with her eyes closed and said nothing.

'Jemima?' he murmured.

'The dirt won't come out,' she said defensively. 'You can get your own supper if it worries you.'

'It's nothing to do with that. Have you got any cream?'

'I want to eat.'

'Have you got any cream?'

'I'll put it on later. I want to eat first so my food doesn't taste of gardenias.'

He let her go, and she bustled about, cutting bread, laying the table, feeding the dogs, making tea—

'Jemima, come and eat.'

She plonked two mugs of tea on the table, sat down and attacked the cheese. He ate his way through a bowl of chicken soup and two doorsteps of bread with slabs of cheese, and watched as she ate at least two bowls of soup and three chunks of bread.

'Where the hell do you put it?' he asked in amazement as she started on a slab of fruitcake.

'No lunch,' she said round a mouthful of cake. 'Have some—your grandmother made it.'

He did, and it was good. Very good. He had more, with another mug of tea, and wondered if the cold or the exercise had sharpened up his appetite.

Finally he ground to a halt, and his hostess took the plates and stacked them by the sink.

'Hands,' he said to her, catching her on the way back from her second trip to the fridge.

'OK.' She reached for some handcream by the sink, ordinary handcream that wouldn't cope with a good bout of spring-cleaning, never mind what she'd been doing, and he took it from her and put it down.

'Antiseptic?'

'What?'

'Antiseptic cream—the sort you put on cuts.'

'Oh.' She opened a cupboard and took some out, and he sat her down, pulled up a chair opposite and spread some into her hands. 'Why are you doing this?' she asked.

He wasn't sure. He didn't tell her that. He didn't say anything, just rubbed the cream gently into the sore fingers until it was all absorbed, then put more on. 'Got anything tougher than that?' he asked, tipping his head towards the handcream.

'No. Well, only the bag balm that we use for cracked udders. It's in the barn, on the shelf by the door. That might do something.'

'I'll get it.'

'Tomorrow will do—'

He stood up and put her hands back on her lap. 'I'll get it,' he repeated, and pulled on his coat and boots. He took the torch, leaving her with the lantern, and went across the yard to the barn. The snow was still flying horizontally, but whether it was fresh snow or just drifting he couldn't tell. Whatever, it was freezing and he was glad to reach the shelter of the barn, cows or not.

It was warm inside, comparatively, warm and full of soft rustlings and sleepy grunts, and the grinding of teeth as they chewed the cud. One of them—Bluebell?—came up and sniffed at him cautiously, and he held out his hand and she licked it, her tongue rough and curiously gentle.

Perhaps cows weren't all bad, he thought, and scratched her face. She watched him for a moment before backing off and rejoining the others, and he thought her eyes were like Jemima's—huge and soft and wary.

He found the cream on the shelf where she'd said, and went back across the Siberian wasteland to the welcoming light from the kitchen window.

It really was bitterly cold in the wind, even colder than it had been an hour before, or perhaps it was because he wasn't working. He went into the lobby, shucked his coat and boots and opened the kitchen door.

She was asleep, curled up in the chair by the fire, Noodle on her lap, Jess at her feet, and he stood there for a moment enjoying the warmth and watched her. Did she need her sleep more than the cream? If she did, would she even wake up if he just put it on?

He unscrewed the lid, eased one of her hands out from under the little white dog and smeared a dollop of cream onto the palm of her hand. She mumbled something in her sleep, and then went quiet again, and he massaged the cream into the cracks and fissures of her hands while Noodle sniffed the cream and went back to sleep.

She didn't move again, just lay there with her head on one side, propped against the wing of the chair, while her chest rose and fell evenly in sleep.

She was exhausted, he realised. Exhausted, overworked and under-funded even without the snow and the power cut.

What would she have done without him?

Coped, was the answer. He knew that, just as he knew he couldn't have left her to fend for herself alone.

He made more tea and drank it, sitting in the other chair by the fire, Jess leaning on his leg while he fondled her ears and watched Jemima sleeping and thought how gutsy she was and what a contrast with the superficial and fickle women he dealt with in his normal daily life.

She had that pioneering spirit that had conquered the Wild West, he thought—grit and determination and sheer bloody-mindedness, coupled with resourcefulness and humour.

Interesting.

It was a shame they were going to be so busy that he wouldn't have time to get to know her!

* * *

Jemima woke at midnight, a crick in her neck and Sam asleep in the easy chair opposite her. She watched him for a moment, enjoying the sight of him stretched out in front of the Rayburn, legs crossed at the ankle, his dark hair tousled and boyish above those sinful black lashes.

He had good bones, she thought idly—good bones and stamina. She pushed Noodle onto the floor, opened the little fire-door in the front of the Rayburn and shovelled in coke and slag to keep it on overnight.

The last thing they needed was that going out!

Sam stirred and mumbled something, and she looked down at him and wondered what she would have done if he hadn't stayed.

Coped, of course, but only just barely and not for long. A day? Two, maybe? No more than that.

She reached out and shook him gently, with a hand that no longer hurt.

'Sam? Time for bed.'

His eyes flew open and locked with hers, and the message in them was warm and sleepy and unmistakable. Then he smiled, a lazy, sexy smile that made her pulse hammer and her mouth go dry as he unfolded out of the chair with a groan.

'I don't suppose you meant that the way it sounded,' he said regretfully, and a smile played around his eyes, taking away any offence.

She smiled back. 'No—I wouldn't have the energy.'

'I wouldn't notice—I'd be asleep.'

They laughed softly, and she put the dogs out for a moment before heading up the stairs. It was much colder in the bedrooms, and she hoped he was a tough and hardy type, or he'd freeze to bits. She remembered her first taste of winter here. It had taken a bit of getting used to, but she'd managed.

'You're in here,' she told him, and pushed the door open. The bed looked neat, the room quite welcoming, but it was cold. 'I'm sorry it's not warmer. I'll get you some extra blankets. If you leave the door open the heat'll come up from the kitchen.'

She reached into the airing cupboard, pulled out a couple of blankets from the bottom and handed them to him. 'I'll leave the lantern here—don't flush the loo, because we haven't got any water. I'll get some buckets in the morning. Anything else you need?'

He shook his head.

'Right, I'll see you in the morning.'

'What time's milking?'

'Five, usually.'

His jaw sagged slightly, then he nodded. 'Wake me.'

'I can manage—'

'Just do it.'

She smiled. He wanted to be a hero? Fine, he could be a hero. 'See you at five, then. Goodnight, Sam—and thanks.'

She went into her room, leaving the door ajar so she had some light, and changed quickly into her pyjamas. Her teeth were scrubbed in a dribble of water, she wiped her face with a cleansing pad and dragged a brush through her hair, then curled up under the covers, rubbing her feet inside the thick bedsocks to keep them warm.

Five o'clock was going to come awfully soon...

Sam was freezing. He pulled on a sweater over his one pair of 'just-in-case' pyjamas, put on a second pair of socks and threw the other blanket over the bed before huddling back under the covers and shuddering with cold.

He must be even more spoilt and pampered than he'd realised.

The wind rattled the window, shaking the glass in the frame and swirling cold air round the room. So much for the warmth coming up from the kitchen!

He tucked his face under the blankets and blew on his hands, trying to warm them, but all he managed to do was make the bed tepid and damp. In the end he tucked the blankets round his head, curled up in a ball and lay still.

There were no night sounds other than the wind. It was strange. He'd stayed with his grandparents just down the road in the summer once, and he could remember the sounds of the night—the owls hooting, the rustling of countless little animals—he'd used to sit on the windowsill and listen to them, and try and imagine what they all were.

His bed dipped, and something cold and wet pushed into his face. His eyelids flew up and his mouth opened to yell when a loud purr echoed round his head.

A cat.

Dammit, he'd nearly died of fright! It nudged him again, and he reached out a hand and scratched its ears and chuckled, the tension draining out of him. A cat he could cope with. It curled up against his chest, and after a moment the purring slowed down and stopped. The warmth seeped through against his chest, and, seconds later, he was asleep.

It was light when he woke—light with the sort of brightness that only happens with a full moon on snow. He shoved the cat out of the way, got stiffly out of bed and went to the window, peering at his watch.

Five-thirty—and there was a light in the barn, a thin sliver of yellow seeping round the sliding door. He pulled on his clothes in the moonlight and limped down the stairs, hideously aware of every muscle, to find a note from Jemima propped up against a mug on the table.

'Gone fishing,' it said. 'Didn't want to disturb the cat.'

He smiled and put the kettle on. However busy she was, she'd have time to sip a cup of tea. The Rayburn needed revving up, and he studied the controls for a minute and decided that it probably needed some breakfast. He found logs in the lobby and pushed them through the little door of the firebox, and once it was packed he opened the vent to allow more air in.

The dogs watched him uninterestedly. Was he eating? No. Therefore they might as well sleep, curled up on the twin chairs. He scooped Noodle up and sat down, and she washed him vigorously before settling down again on his lap.

It reminded him that he needed a shave, but water was short and a beard might keep his face warm in the wind.

Not that it would have much chance to grow before the power came back on, whenever that might be. He put Noodle down and went into the parlour to phone the electricity board.

Still no further news, except that it would be some time and thousands of homes were out. He fiddled with a little radio on the kitchen windowsill and found a local station, which told him that a helicopter had flown into some power lines in the blizzard and knocked out half of Dorset.

So, still hand-milking, then—and hauling the water. Great.

The kettle boiled and he made tea, pulled on his coat and boots and went out. It was cold and crisp, his breath making little puffs on the bright moonlit air, but the wind had dropped and the sun would be creeping over the horizon in an hour or so. Strange how fickle February could be.

He trudged across the yard towards the barn, slid the door back and was greeted with a smile that warmed him down to the bottom of his boots.

'My hero!' she said with a laugh, and she got stiffly to her feet, pressed her hands into the small of her back and stretched, giving a little groan.

'Sore?'

'Am I ever. I thought I was fit. How about you?'

He grinned. 'Oh, I can feel muscles I didn't know I had.' He gave her her tea. 'How are the hands?'

'Better.' She smiled ruefully. 'I never really thanked you—I fell asleep while you were doing it.'

'It's my magic touch—and anyway, you were already asleep.'

'I wonder why?' She buried her nose in her mug and drank a huge gulp of tea, then sighed. 'Gorgeous. I was dying for tea. I thought I might finish the cows and come and get some, but they're being really awkward. They just won't let down for me this morning. I don't think the water's very warm any more, that's the trouble.'

He drained his mug. 'I'll get you some. I put the kettle back on the hob.'

'You're just a regular sweetheart. Remind me to thank Mary for lending you to me.'

He leant back against the wall, arms folded. 'Just as a matter of interest,' he said slowly, 'where is their farm?'

She coloured slightly. 'Over the hill.'

'About three or four hundred yards?'

'Something like that.'

'So I could have got there last night.'

To her credit she met his eyes. 'Possibly.'

He smiled slowly. 'Just think,' he said, 'what I might have missed.'

Something sad and a little desperate happened to her eyes. 'Yes, just think. You could still have been in bed now.' She handed him her mug. 'Better get on.'

He went back to the kitchen, filled the bucket with hot water and poured her another mug of tea. She'd drunk the first almost in one gulp. He wondered why she'd looked sad when he'd talked about getting to his grandparents. Did she think he'd go? And leave her, with this lot to do?

She didn't know him very well, he thought, picking up the tea and the bucket. After he'd delivered them he carried water into the house, some to the kitchen, some to the bathroom, and then he went back to the barn.

'Fill the troughs?' he suggested.

She looked at him in amazement. 'Aren't you going?'

'Without my car? You have to be kidding,' he joked, but she nodded, as if she thought it was perfectly reasonable.

'In which case…'

Hope flickered in her amber eyes, and if he'd cherished any illusions about being able to escape, they evaporated like mist in the early morning. He couldn't abandon her—and if he did, his grandmother would kick him straight back down here again before he was even over the threshold!

'I'll fill the troughs,' he said, and wondered why the thought of shifting a hundred and fifty buckets of water made him want to whistle…

CHAPTER THREE

THE dawn, when it came, was glorious. The wind had gone, the sun sparkled on the snow and if she hadn't been so phenomenally tired Jemima would have loved it.

Sam, for all his bucketing, seemed full of energy this morning, and she wanted to hit him for it. She'd listened to him whistling cheerfully as he brought the water up from the stream—seventy-five times, or thereabouts—and now he was shovelling snow away from the barn doors and making paths from the house to the hens, the calves and the stream.

Still, she wasn't surprised. As a boy he'd never sat still for a minute. 'There's some sand somewhere you can put down on those paths,' she told him, sticking her head out of the hen house.

He looked round at the farmyard. Snow had come straight off the field across the road and dumped itself on the yard, and Jemima took one look at his expression and hid a grin.

'Any helpful suggestions where I should start looking?' he said mildly.

'Ah.' She gave up and grinned. 'How about ash from the bottom of the Rayburn?' she offered.

His expression cleared. 'Good idea. Got a metal bucket?'

'By the back door—it's got ash in it. If you're going in, could you take these?'

She handed him a basket of eggs and he peered at

them and cocked his head on one side with a quizzical grin. 'I wonder what's for breakfast?' he murmured.

She laughed. 'Put the kettle on, too. We'll do the paths together in a minute.'

She ducked back inside the hen house, collected and packed the last of the eggs and checked the water, then shut them up and went across to the house. She wondered when he'd remember who she was, if he ever did, and decided to let it go on a bit longer before saying anything. It made the day more interesting, waiting for the penny to drop, she thought as she kicked off her boots.

The warmth wrapped itself round her like a blanket as she went in, and she dropped into a chair by the Rayburn and propped her feet on the front edge. 'Oh, bliss,' she groaned, and shut her eyes.

A hard, lean, masculine hip nudged her ankles. 'Come on, out of the way. I'm trying to cook.'

She cracked an eye open. 'Cook?' she said disbelievingly.

'Cook. Put some handcream on and keep out of the way. Is there any butter?'

She got up and found butter, then milk, then cut some bread and put it in the toaster.

'When did you intend to have breakfast?' he asked drily, and she muttered and flipped the bread back out of the lifeless tool and plopped back into the chair.

'We'll have bread,' she suggested, and he laughed, turning those astonishing navy eyes on her so her heart hiccuped. Wow, she thought, if he really set out to be charming he could be a real stunner—

'How do you like your eggs?'

'Soft and creamy.'

'Ditto. Right, up you get.'

She was suddenly ravenous. The heap of rich, golden scrambled egg was cooked to perfection, and she stabbed her fork into it, forgetting all about Sam and his gorgeous dark blue eyes.

Sam watched her dive headfirst into her eggs and smiled a very masculine and self-satisfied smile. He felt a strange surge of protective warmth, and the smile faded. Protective warmth? What the hell was he on about?

He stabbed the egg but it was too soft to co-operate and he had to scoop instead—not nearly so satisfying. He shot his chair back and almost snatched his mug off the table. 'More tea?' he growled, and her head flew up, eyes wide with surprise.

'Did I say something to upset you?' she asked mildly.

He sighed. 'No. More tea?' he repeated, in a softer tone, and she held out her mug.

'Thanks.'

He paused at the window, then set the mugs down on the draining board. There was a man coming up the path, tall and broad and rugged-looking, and he felt the hairs go up on the back of his neck. 'You've got a visitor,' he growled.

'A visitor?' She stood up and came to the window beside him, going up on tiptoe to see.

'Damn. It's Owen.'

'Owen?'

She went to the door, just as a loud knock set the dogs off. He hung back, just for a moment, reminding himself that it really wasn't his business who came calling at Jemima's door.

'Morning, Jemima,' a voice sounded cheerfully. 'Thought I'd better come and make sure you were all right, with the power off and no generator.'

'I'm fine, Owen, thanks,' she said, but Sam couldn't hear much after that because of the dogs. He shut them up by putting his half-finished eggs into their bowls, then went back to the door to eavesdrop.

'Car stuck in the lane,' Owen was saying. 'Someone's tied some saucy underwear to sticks to mark it.'

'It's mine,' Sam said, coming up behind Jemima and trying to loom over Owen. It was difficult, even with Owen on the step below, but he tried anyway, roiling with some primitive instinct that made him want to punch the man's lights out.

Owen looked him up and down, then smiled slowly. 'Yours, eh? Funny, that. Can't see you wearing that sort of gear, but it takes all sorts.'

Sam felt heat brush his neck. 'The car,' he growled. 'Not the underwear.'

'Oh.' Owen looked at Jemima. 'Must be yours, then.'

He could nearly feel the warmth coming off her cheeks and he wanted to flatten Owen for embarrassing her. She mumbled something indistinct about red, and then offered the wretched man a cup of tea.

'Don't mind if I do,' Owen said, stepping in and forcing him to retreat. He was hugely satisfied to see Jess growl at Owen with her hackles up. The dog stationed herself between Jemima and the intruder and let out another low, warning rumble.

Sam had to turn away to hide his grin. He topped up the pot, poured three mugs of tea and wasn't surprised to see Owen shovel four spoons of sugar into his mug. His huge hairy hand enveloped the mug, and he slurped with satisfaction.

Oh, dear.

'So, how're you managing?' Owen asked.

'Oh, all right. Sam's been bucketing the water and I've been milking and feeding the stock—'

'You should have called. I would have come to help; there was no need for you get outsiders in.'

He shot Sam a threatening look, and Sam arched a brow. 'Outsiders?' he said softly.

'Well, you're a city boy, aren't you?' Owen said disparagingly. 'Soft as grease.'

A memory stirred, from long ago in the summer he'd spent with his grandparents. He shot Owen a keen look. 'I remember a boy called Owen from round here. I must have been about eight at the time, and there was a little girl called Gemma or something like that.'

'Jem,' she corrected softly.

His eyes flicked to hers and widened with recognition, and he smiled. 'Jem? That was you? You can't be old enough—you'd have to be—what, twenty-eight now?'

She nodded. 'I wondered if you'd remember.'

The smile widened. 'Oh, yes. You've changed. Grown up—well, a bit. You're still knee-high to a grasshopper, but I didn't recognise you. Don't tell me, I don't look any different!'

'Oh, you do. You're much bigger, for a start. I only worked it out because of Dick and Mary.'

He nodded thoughtfully and his eyes flicked back to Owen. 'Anyway, as I was saying, this lad, Owen, he teased Jem and made her cry, so I hit him.' He studied his mug. 'As I recall, Owen ran home to Mummy in tears.'

Uh-oh. Jemima hid behind her mug, almost burying her face in it. Owen wouldn't like that!

Owen didn't. Owen flushed a dark, angry rust. 'I was just a lad—only a child.'

'And she was even younger.' His smile faded. He was

impatient now to be rid of this bumbling, bullying oaf who was trying to warn him off. 'Don't worry about Jemima, Owen, I'll take care of her. You go on home to Mummy.'

The man banged down his mug and stood up, crossed the kitchen in a single stride and slammed the door. Moments later the outer door shut with a bang, and Jess, hackles slowly subsiding, whimpered and pressed her head into Jemima's hand.

Sam smirked.

It was the wrong thing to do. Jemima set down her cup and shoved back her chair, standing up impatiently. Jess, sensing her irritation, slithered off to cower behind him. 'Why the hell did you have to do that?' she asked in exasperation.

'Do what?'

'You know perfectly well. Don't play the innocent—flexing your muscles at each other like prize fighters. I thought for a minute he was going to hit you.'

'I was ready.'

She snorted. 'You aren't eight any more, and in case you hadn't noticed, he's bigger than you.'

'He's bigger than you, too,' Sam said, suddenly serious. 'Much bigger, and he wants you.'

'Don't be ridiculous, he's just a neighbour.'

Sam made a rude noise.

'He is.'

'In a pig's eye. The man has the hots for you, poppet, and if you can't see it, you're blind.'

She blushed. 'You're wrong.'

'No.'

'He's never done anything—'

'Not yet. What will you do if he does? If he decides

he's been patient long enough and it's time to move things on?'

She laughed uneasily. 'He wouldn't do anything stupid like that—and anyway, how do I know I'm safe with you?'

'Of course you are. You always were—quite apart from which, you've made sure I'm too damn tired to be a threat.'

She looked up at him for a few seconds, then gave a weary laugh. 'OK. Just don't see him off again, all right? He's got a hydraulic shovel on a four-wheel drive tractory thing. It's used for shifting silage and so on, and it makes a really useful snow plough. If you play your cards right he'll get your car out for you and you'll be able to leave.'

'We've already had this conversation. I've said I'm not going.'

'Ever?' she asked in disbelief.

Something strange happened inside Sam, something primitive and basic and elemental, and he turned away and dumped his mug in the sink. He would have to leave her some time, of course, and now he knew she'd be at the mercy of Owen the Ox.

Hell.

There was a sharp creak from overhead, and Jemima raised her head and peered at the barn roof. There it was again.

'What's that?' Sam asked, peering up at the roof too.

'I think the snow's too heavy. I'll have to get up there and try and scrape it off.'

'Over my dead body.'

'It can be arranged.'

He grinned. 'I'm sure. Nevertheless, I'll go up there.'

She felt almost weak with relief. She simply hated heights.

They went outside and looked at the roof. On the side of the lane there was virtually no snow, but where the wind had carried it over the ridge it had settled in curls, like waves caught in the moment of breaking.

'It must weigh tons,' Sam said, eyeing it thoughtfully. 'I wonder what's the best way to get it off?'

'Uncle Tom used to lift the bucket of the tractor up and make me scrape it with a broom, but—'

'Since the tractor's out of use, we can't do that.' He looked round. 'Got a ladder?'

'In the barn.'

They fetched it, and Sam climbed gingerly up to the level of the eaves and peered at the snow. The roof pitch was a little steep to stand on, but the snow would provide some grip. Jemima followed him halfway up the ladder and handed him a broom.

'Here, try this.'

He took it, using it to steady himself as he stepped cautiously up onto the roof. He muttered something she was glad she couldn't hear, then started tentatively prodding at the snow with the broom.

It was useless.

Jemima came down the ladder and stood at the side of the barn, knee-deep in the snow, and tilted her head back to watch him. 'Try hitting it,' she suggested.

'Who's doing this, you or me?'

'I'm quite happy to do it; you know that.'

'You stay where you are. I don't want the barn roof to cave in. I can feel it shifting. Is the snow moving?'

'Not from where I'm standing. I think you need to go a bit further up and thump it with the end of the broom.'

'I'll thump you with the end of the broom. Just let me try it my way.'

'It won't work,' she sang, watching him brushing little patterns all over the top of the snow. 'Just thump it—'

'Oh, for heaven's sake, woman—' He hurled the brush down onto the roof and glared at her, then his face changed.

There was a hissing, slithering sound and, almost in slow motion, the whole side of the roof seemed to slide in one solid mass down over the edge of the barn.

Jemima shrieked and leapt back, and with a wild yell Sam came hurtling towards her, arms and legs cart-wheeling wildly. She tripped and fell backwards, Sam crashed into her and then the snow poured down around them and almost smothered them.

There was a second of stunned silence, then she said victoriously, 'I told you you needed to thump it.'

Sam looked down at her face, just inches away, and debated strangling her to get the triumphant grin off those impudent little lips. He went one better. He brushed the snow off her eyebrow, lowered his head and kissed the smile away.

He'd wanted to do it twenty-two years ago, but he hadn't had the nerve. Now, all those years later and with the threat of Owen looming over them like the north face of the Eiger, he suddenly found the courage.

For a moment she didn't move, frozen under him, and he wondered if he'd misjudged the look in her eyes, but then her thigh shifted against his groin, her arms came up round him and with a groan of satisfaction he threaded his fingers through her hair, coaxed her lips apart and plundered that delectable little mouth.

His heart jerked and then started to thunder, and there was a massive roaring in his ears.

So massive that the earth seemed to move…

He lifted his head a fraction, staring at her in amazement. Was Hemingway right? Good Lord! He was glad he hadn't tried kissing her twenty-two years ago; it would have blown his brains out—

'You all right?'

His head snapped up. He glared over his shoulder at Owen and staggered to his feet, shaking off the ton or so of snow that had fallen on them. The earthshaking focused on a huge yellow machine at the entrance to the yard. Not Hemingway, then. Pity. His mouth tightened.

'Fine, thanks. Aren't you busy?'

'Yeah—just clearing the lane. Thought you might want to get your things—your car'll be out in a minute, so you can leave.'

'I'm staying,' he said defiantly, and met the challenge in Owen's eyes with one of his own.

Owen turned away. 'We'll see,' he said softly, and stomped back out of the yard.

Behind him Sam could hear Jemima struggling to her feet, and he turned to her and pulled her up. 'Sorry about that.'

'What—the kiss, or Owen?'

He smiled ruefully. 'I meant falling off the roof and landing on you.'

'Oh, that.' She laughed, and banged at the snow on her jeans. 'It needed to come down. Are you hurt?'

'No. You?'

He looked at her, so fragile and feisty, eyes sparkling, hair wildly tangled and filled with snow, and felt sick at the thought of her being injured.

'I'm fine.'

'I landed on you.'

She smiled. 'I noticed. You've got more muscles than I realised.'

He felt colour brush his neck and stepped back before he did something stupid. 'I'll find my car keys. Can I put the car on the yard?'

'Yes, but I should clear a space. On second thoughts I'll ask Owen to clear it while he's got the snow plough here.'

She did, and Sam watched in frustration as his neatly cleared paths that had taken hours of back-breaking work were casually swept out of the way with a couple of swipes from Owen's fancy gadget.

Damn the man.

She gave him a cup of tea, as well, after he'd towed Sam's car out of the snow drift with a few well-chosen words and an effortless tug from the yellow monster.

'Smart car,' he said with a nod to the almost new BMW. 'Be all right in the city.'

Then he wandered off, hands in pockets, whistling, to have tea with Jemima while Sam struggled to reverse his car up the slippery lane and into the yard. There were flowers in the back seat for his grandmother, and he scooped them up. They'd brighten the kitchen, anyway, and it might put a spoke in Owen's wheel.

He locked the car, went into the kitchen and was greeted with huge enthusiasm by Jess, who came and sat beside him and growled at Owen.

'Good girl,' Sam said, fondling her ears, and Jemima gave him a dirty look. He smiled innocently. He could enjoy this. After all, he was one up on Owen. He'd kissed her this morning.

He handed her the flowers he'd bought for his grandmother, producing them from behind his back with a flourish. Owen goggled, Jemima's eyes widened and then went misty, and he wished he'd actually bought them for her.

'You aren't going to tell me you just had these delivered,' she said with suspicion, and he smiled wryly.

'I could always lie. They were for my grandmother. I thought you might enjoy them.'

'Whatever next? Daft bloody nonsense,' Owen muttered. He got to his feet, put his mug in the sink and then, with a defiant glare at Sam, he bent over and dropped a kiss on Jemima's startled lips.

'Give us a shout if you need anything. We'll give you a hand, you know that—and if you decide the herd's too much, we can always take them up to ours and milk them. We've got the standby generator.'

'We'll manage,' Sam ground out, furious with Owen for daring to defile Jemima's lips.

Jemima glowered at him, then turned a sweet smile on the other man. 'Thank you, Owen, you're very kind. I'll think about it, if the power's off for much longer.'

'Of course, you could always do the sensible thing and sell me the herd.'

Sam got to his feet.

'Weren't you just leaving?' he said softly, bristling, and Jemima glowered at him again.

Owen arched a brow, sketched a farewell salute to Jemima and went out, banging the door again. Jess growled, whined and ran to Jemima, licking her hands furiously.

'I don't think she thinks much of your suitor,' he said with a grin.

'I don't think much of either of you,' she retorted, dumping the flowers in a bucket of water to recover from their dry night. 'Squabbling over me like a couple of fighting cocks. It's ridiculous.'

'You didn't mind when you were six.'

'I was a foolish child,' she retorted. 'I was impressed by your bravado—and anyway, your grandmother made better cakes than Owen's mother.'

He laughed. 'I expect she still does.'

'She does—but my judgement's a little more sophisticated now.'

Sam made a non-committal noise. Anyone who would allow Owen the Ox on the premises in his opinion was showing particularly poor judgement, but obviously only Jess agreed with him.

'Haven't you got something to do?' he groused, mightily ticked off that she was still defending Owen.

'Yes—the mucking out. Want to lend a hand—seeing as you insist on staying? You might as well make yourself useful.'

He ground his teeth to hold back the retort and followed her out. He could think of plenty of ways of making himself useful around her, and mucking out wasn't one of them...

He was useful, she had to admit that. She could hardly remember him from twenty-two years ago, but she could remember that the summer he was there had been brighter than the others.

They'd laughed a lot, giggling over all sorts of things, and she could remember Owen sulking and grumbling because she'd always been his exclusive preserve until Sam had come along.

She'd forgotten all about it until he'd mentioned the fight with Owen. Then it had all come flooding back, and she wondered why she hadn't remembered the animosity between them before.

Come to think of it, she wondered why she hadn't recognised him at first.

Perhaps because after twenty-two years he'd changed?

She laughed softly to herself. Of course he'd changed—outwardly, at least. He was still squabbling with Owen, though. Her smile faded, replaced by a frown, and she looked round at the plump, mottled brown cows that had been Uncle Tom's pride and joy.

Owen kept on offering to buy them, but she wasn't sure if it was just an excuse to come and visit her or if he really wanted them. It was irrelevant, either way, because they were her livelihood and she had no intention of parting with them either for love or money—and anyway, she didn't love Owen and never would.

He just did nothing for her at all.

Unlike Sam.

She paused in the middle of forking up the fresh straw to look across at him. He'd cleared his half of the barn and was fossicking about at the far end, near the vacuum pump that powered the milking machine.

His shoulders were broader than she'd realised, and he wasn't soft. At least, he hadn't felt soft when he'd landed on her. She thought of the kiss, so fleeting and not nearly long enough, and stifled a moan.

He was just passing through. She didn't need trouble like that. If he was right about Owen, and she had a feeling he was, she had more than enough on her plate already.

'Jem? Come and have a look at this.'

He was crouched with his back to her, fiddling with something, and as she watched he pivoted on his foot and beckoned to her.

'What?'

'This Lister engine. What's it for?'

'What Lister engine?'

She propped her fork up at the side of the barn and went over to him. He was using his sleeve to scrub at a little metal plate on the greasy, dusty pile of redundant junk that he'd found under an old tarpaulin.

'One and a half horse power,' he told her, and looked at the vacuum pump nearby. 'It's bolted to the ground. Do you suppose it used to be used to drive the milking machine?'

She studied it, imagining it clean, and a memory stirred.

'Could be. Do you suppose we could make it work?'

'Don't know. It needs a belt. The electric motor's got a V-belt but this needs a flat one.'

She shrugged. 'I wouldn't know.'

'Got any spare belts about?'

'Got one on my jeans.'

He laughed and straightened up. 'Not that sort of belt, Jem.' He scanned the wall of the barn. 'More—that sort.'

He pointed to a flat, wide loop festooned with cobwebs, dangling on the wall with a handful of chains and old baler twine.

'I wonder…'

He went and hooked it down, dusted it off and held it up to the machine. It was the right length. 'Looks like a spare that never got used,' he murmured, examining it.

'Can you change it? Or get the engine started?' she asked doubtfully, looking at the dusty, grubby engine with no great hope. It would be wonderful if he could, but she didn't dare get her hopes up—

'I'll give it a whirl. I'll need some petrol.'

'In the tractor shed.'

'What is wrong with the tractor, by the way?' he asked. 'Perhaps I could fix that?'

She coloured. 'I doubt it. The engine block's cracked—I forgot to put antifreeze into it.'

'Oops.' He hid the smile valiantly, but she knew it was there. She was tempted to kick him, but he was just about to try and fix the milking machine up to the little engine, and she wasn't suicidally stupid.

'I'll get the petrol,' she said hastily, and went out, hoping there was a good supply. There should be—she usually had a couple of cans just to be on the safe side, because the lawn mower ran on petrol and the old Fergie tractor had a petrol starter—but there was always the possibility she'd had to put it in her car and had forgotten to fill it up.

She was in luck. There were two almost full cans, and she took them back to Sam.

'Hopeful, aren't you?' he said with an arched brow, and poured some into the little tank. 'Water?'

'Water?'

'It has a tank here for water,' he explained, pointing to an oval hole in the top of the machine.

She fetched clean water and he filled the tank. Then he stood up, grasped hold of the little crank handle and yanked.

'Ah.'

She eyed him, sitting on the clean straw, the broken handle dangling from his fingers, and hid a smile. 'That's a good omen,' she said drily.

He took a nice, deep breath and said nothing. She thought he was probably counting to ten before he spoke.

'Got a crank handle for the tractor?' he asked calmly, getting to his feet and dusting off his bottom.

'Yes.'

'Does it work?'

'Well, not at the moment. I told you the tractor's out of action.'

'I don't want the tractor; I want the handle. I don't suppose you could lay your hands on it?'

'Do you think it will fit?' she asked, amazed at his resourcefulness.

'No—I was going to use it to club you to death—'

She put her fists on her hips. 'No need to get sarky,' she chided.

'I want the handle,' he explained, patiently, as if he was talking to a particularly stupid child, 'to replace this broken one.'

'I'll get it. It's in the tractor shed.'

'Got any tools?'

'In the workshop. Uncle Tom had all sorts of things.'

'Good. Right, let's have a look.'

She showed him where everything was, offered to help and then made herself scarce after the crank handle had slipped off the end of the shaft for the third time.

'I'll—ah—be in the kitchen if you need me,' she told him, and, taking a bucket of fresh milk, she headed out of the barn and left him to it.

She made a rice pudding, an egg custard, put some milk to stand to skim the cream off and then wondered if she ought to make clotted cream with all the stuff in the cooling tank in the barn. She'd never done it, but Mary might know.

She rang her.

'Oh, hello, Jemima,' she said cheerfully. 'Is Sam being useful, dear?'

'Wonderfully. Thank you for giving him to me.'

Mary laughed. 'You're most welcome. A little exercise will do him good. He spends far too much time indoors.'

'Not at the moment. He's struggling to fix an engine. Mary, I've got a problem. I've got gallons of milk all settling out in the tank, and there's a huge thick layer of cream on the top. I was thinking I could make clotted cream with it, but I don't know how. Got any idea?'

She did, of course, and so Jemima prepared all the pans, fetched some of the cream from the holding tank and stuck her head into the barn. 'How's it going?'

'Don't ask,' he growled.

She retreated to her kitchen out of the way, skimming and scalding and potting and generally feeling terribly pleased with herself, and then while the cream cooled she made some fruit scones to have with the cream and dug out the last pot of Mary's strawberry jam.

'Lunch,' she said with satisfaction, ignoring the fact that it was three in the afternoon.

She pulled on her boots, opened the back door and stopped dead in amazement.

From the barn she could hear an engine running.

True, it was spluttering and coughing, and after a minute or so it died, but it had started! Thrilled to bits with the prospect of the milking machine back in action, she ran across the yard and went smack into Sam's chest.

She stepped back, laughing, and looked up into his gorgeous navy eyes. 'It works!' she exclaimed.

He smiled smugly, but she let him get away with it. Apart from the fact that she was so pleased with him, he had a streak of oil across his unshaven face, his hands were black to the wrist and he looked piratical and sexy and happier than he'd looked since he'd arrived.

Then she noticed his knuckle dribbling blood.

'You've cut yourself!' she cried softly, taking his hand in hers.

He shrugged. 'I knocked it on the floor when the crank handle flew off. Come and see. It's not perfect—it probably needs stripping down—but I think it'll be OK.'

It was. The belt fitted, the engine ran—and the vacuum pump didn't work. 'The damn belt's slipping,' he muttered, glaring at it.

'Want some treacle?'

He looked at her as if she were a few sandwiches short of a picnic. 'Why the hell would I want treacle?' he growled.

'To make the belt sticky. Uncle Tom used to use it. It's up there.'

He looked up, and there was an ancient, rusting pot of treacle on a high shelf in between an old can of paint and a collection of crumpled rags.

'Treacle,' he murmured, and, reaching the tin down, he prised the lid off, smeared a little on the belt and started the little engine again.

It worked.

He turned to her with a grin. 'There you go, I've fixed your milking machine,' he said with a beaming smile, and to her absolute astonishment she burst into tears.

'Jemima?'

She sniffed and turned away. 'Sorry. I'm just being silly. It reminded me of Uncle Tom.'

A firm, heavy hand closed over her shoulder and squeezed comfortingly. 'How about a cup of tea?' he suggested.

She nodded and sniffed, scrubbing her nose on the back of her hand. 'I'll go and make it.'

He cut the engine, wiped his hands on a rag and straightened up.

'You should put a plaster on that,' she told him, looking at his bloodied knuckle and sniffing again.

'I'll let you.'

'So kind.'

His stomach rumbled. 'I don't suppose there's any chance of anything to eat?' he said hopefully.

'Oh, I might let you have a dry crust—since you've fixed the engine.'

They kicked off their boots and went into the kitchen, and Sam's eyes widened. 'Scones and clotted cream?' he said in awe, and she laughed.

'And rice pudding and egg custard in the oven. Basically, if it's got eggs, milk or cream in it, it's on the menu.'

He grinned. 'Suits me.' It did. It suited him to the tune of three cups of tea, eight scones and most of the cream.

'I take it you don't worry about cholesterol?' she said with a chuckle, watching him lick the last trace of cream off those smooth, full lips.

'That would be churlish, since you've gone to so much trouble.' His smile warmed her all the way down to her toes.

'I really am grateful about the engine,' she told him. 'The cows definitely don't like being hand-milked.'

'My pleasure. I like fixing things.'

She nodded. 'I suppose you'll go now. Your car's out, I can cope with the milking—'

'How about the water?'

She straightened her spine. 'I can manage the water.'

'I dare say—but I'd hate to give Owen the Ox a chance to be valiant.'

She laughed, ridiculously relieved because yet again he didn't seem to be about to desert her.

'In that case,' she said with a smile, 'I'll go and start the milking and you can carry buckets!'

CHAPTER FOUR

'TELL me about your cows.'

Jemima pulled the last suction cup off Ruby's udder and straightened up with the bucket. 'My cows? Well, they're pedigree Dairy Shorthorns, and as you can see they look like fat Fresians but mottled brown instead of black and white, and they have generally less milk than Fresians but it's a better quality.'

'And Owen wants them.'

She snorted and moved on to the next cow, washing her udder and slipping the suction cups on the cluster onto each clean pink teat in turn. The milk flowed through the clear pipe with satisfying ease, and she sighed with relief.

'Yes, Owen wants them. I think.'

'You think?'

'He's—always here. You might be right,' she conceded grudgingly.

'I am right.'

'Are you always right?'

He grinned. 'Usually.'

'Once I thought I was wrong, but I was mistaken,' she mumbled under her breath, but he heard and laughed.

'Listen, Jem, I'm only human. I just know that when a man has that look in his eye, his mind is fixed below his belt. He may want your cows, but as sure as eggs he wants you, too.'

She coloured. She could feel the warmth flooding her

cheeks, but she couldn't look away because Sam was looking at her with that self-same look in his eyes and she was transfixed by it.

It was only the empty slurping noise of the vacuum pump that dragged her attention off him and back to the job in hand. Confused, torn between thumping him for his cocky impudence and throwing herself into his arms, she turned back to the cows and steadfastly ignored him.

He wouldn't be ignored, though, following her and quizzing her, asking all sorts of daft questions until in the end she jackknifed up and glared at him.

'Have you done the water?' she snapped, and he closed his mouth into a hard line and backed away.

'I'll do it now,' he said tightly, and she felt a wash of shame. He was helping her out of the kindness of his heart, after all, and she had no business speaking to him like that. Heavens, she wouldn't speak to him like that if she employed him, never mind the fact that he was just an unwilling volunteer!

She ran after him, catching up with him as he swung the first bucket into the river.

'Sam, I'm sorry.'

He stopped, bucket suspended in mid-air, then lowered it slowly to the ground. It slopped over and settled. 'Were you always a spoilt little brat or did that happen after you were six?'

She felt the heat in her cheeks and made herself hold his eyes. 'You were crowding me. I'm not used to it. I've been working alone for a year.' She looked down and scuffed the ash with her toe. 'I know that's no excuse for being so rude. I don't know why you haven't left.'

There was a long pause.

'Nor do I,' he said eventually. 'Do you want me to?'

'No.' She shook her head almost violently. 'Oh, no. I need your help. I thought I could cope, and for a day or so maybe I could, but it looks as if this power cut will go on for ages.' She dragged in a steadying breath. 'I could ask Owen—'

He bit out a terse and very to the point remark, and she smiled to herself.

'I take it you don't think I should ask Owen.'

'Too bloody right.' He hooked up another bucket and swung it into the water, pulled it out and retrieved the first from by her feet. 'Ask Owen and I guarantee he'll want payment in kind.'

'The cows?'

'Or you. He's probably not that bothered either way.'

She fell into step beside him. 'And you?'

'What about me?'

'How do you want paying?'

He set the buckets down. 'Who the hell said anything about paying me?'

'There's no such thing as a free lunch.'

He closed his eyes and snorted. 'I'm helping you because my grandmother would have my hide if I didn't.'

She felt a little stab of disappointment. 'Oh.'

'What?'

'Nothing. I'll get on with the milking.'

She finished in half the time it had taken that morning, despite the Lister engine running out of petrol and being difficult to start again. Sam struggled with it, though, and she stripped out Daisy while she was waiting.

The satisfaction of tipping out the last bucket of milk before she was quite dead on her feet was amazing. She went out, lantern in hand, and found Sam just finishing off the water for the calves.

'All done?'

He nodded. 'You?'

'Yes. They've got hay for the night. Sam?'

'Yes?'

'Thank you.'

He was silent for a long time, then he smiled, a crooked, fleeting little smile. 'My pleasure.'

'Liar.'

The smile widened. 'My privilege, then.'

'Some privilege.'

They fell into step towards the house. 'You know what you were saying about the free lunch?'

She laughed. 'Don't tell me—you're hungry.'

'Starving. Have you got any real food?'

'In the freezer. It's probably still frozen as it's out in the porch. What do you fancy?'

He grinned. 'Not beef or chicken.'

She thought of the scant contents of her freezer. 'You may be out of luck.'

He was. She had a couple of chicken portions, half a pound of minced beef, six fish fingers and a little heap of ice, peas and bits of plastic bag.

'Don't tell me,' he said, eyeing the interior with jaundice, 'you were going shopping today.'

She chuckled. 'Maybe. It usually looks pretty grim.'

He cast an eye up to the sky. The moon was out, almost full, and with the snow it was cold but bright.

'We could walk over to my grandparents.'

'They won't have anything.'

'They might. Grannie's always got a casserole on the go and she was expecting me.'

The thought of real food was almost enough to make her cry. 'All right—but ring her first.'

He disappeared into the parlour with a lamp, and came back a minute later grinning broadly. 'She's just heating it up. She'd cooked up a storm because I was coming for the weekend. I said we'd be over in a trice. She told me to bring clean clothes—we can have a bath.'

'A hot bath?'

'Yes—the Aga's under the water tank.'

'Oh, wow. Real water.'

He laughed. 'Indeed. Come on, then, or it'll be midnight before we get there.'

They gathered their things together, whistled up the dogs and set off up the field. It was bitterly cold even though there was no wind, and they had to carry Noodle because she was shivering. Jess, though, was off, streaking away over the field and waiting for them by the Aga when they arrived.

The smell of home cooking assailed their nostrils as they went in, and Mary welcomed them with open arms and huge hugs, exclaiming with delight over the clotted cream Jemima had brought her. Dick was less effusive, but equally pleased to see them, and Jemima could tell from the look in his eye how fond he was of Sam.

'I'm sorry I've stolen him when he should be staying with you,' Jemima apologised.

'Nonsense,' Mary said, flapping her hand and bustling to the stove. 'What do you want first? Brandy, cup of tea, hot bath or stew?'

'Brandy,' Sam said without hesitation.

'Tea in the bath.'

Sam laughed. 'Typical woman. I bet you'll be hours.'

She was, but only because she went to sleep out of sheer exhaustion. She was woken by Sam tapping on the door. 'Come on, it's my turn.'

She mumbled something rude and climbed out, swathed herself in the towel Mary had given her and opened the door. 'You,' she told him firmly, 'are a bully.'

'I also have it on good authority that I need a bath.'

She sniffed and nodded. 'Yup. Definite aroma of cow.'

'Well, come on, then, out of the way.'

She scooped up her clothes and went into the nearest bedroom to dress, then ran downstairs with her dirty clothes in a bag and her wet hair dangling in rats' tails round her face. Dick pressed a brandy into her hand, Mary thanked her again for the clotted cream and she sat there under the bathroom and couldn't think about anything except Sam overhead wallowing naked in the bath.

She got lost halfway through a sentence and Mary and Dick exchanged speaking glances. 'Sorry, I'm tired,' she mumbled.

'Has it been very difficult?'

She looked at Mary's kindly face. 'Not with Sam's help. Without, it would have been impossible.'

'How convenient, then, that he was here.'

'You lied to him.'

Mary smiled. 'Only a little. It is two miles by road because you have to go up to the village.'

'Don't apologise. I'm hugely grateful.'

'Dick, I think we need more logs on the fire in the sitting room, dear.'

Dick stood up dutifully and went out to check, and Mary reached over and covered Jemima's hand with her own soft, smooth one. 'How are you getting on?'

She laughed softly. 'He's jealous of Owen.'

'He always was. I was trying to work it out. I think it must have been about twenty-two years ago you were both here at the same time.'

'It was. I'd forgotten how much they hated each other until he and Owen almost came to blows in the kitchen.'

'Oh, how exciting! Nobody's fought over me for years.'

Jemima chuckled. 'Mary, it was awful. They were squabbling like starlings.'

'It's a good sign, though. He wouldn't squabble if he wasn't interested.'

'But I don't want him to be interested!' she said, just as Sam came back into the room.

'You talking about Owen again?' he growled, and Mary leapt in before she could say a word.

'Jemima tells me he's being a nuisance.'

'I said no such thing,' she protested, eyeing his neatly slicked wet hair and clean-shaven cheeks. Funny, she preferred him scruffy and a little wild. 'He's being very useful.'

'Flashing his gadget about, anyway,' Sam grumbled.

'You're just jealous because you haven't got one,' Jemima said, and he chuckled.

'I don't need a telescopic ram to impress the ladies,' he bragged, and Mary swatted him.

'Come on, let's get some food into you. At least you smell a bit better now. Leave your dirty things here and I'll wash them for you. Now, about this supper…'

They set off a little before midnight, stuffed to the gills and singing their heads off after all the brandy Dick had coaxed down them, and they would have been all right if Sam hadn't stumbled over a hidden log by the ditch and fallen headlong into six feet of snow.

Jemima dragged him out, laughing helplessly, and he promptly fell back in again, pulling her after him. She landed on his chest, sprawled over his body with their legs intimately aligned, and the laughter left them.

'Jem?' he murmured, lifting a hand to brush her hair back from her face, and in the moonlight she could see the question in his eyes.

If she kissed him—if she just lowered her head and touched her lips to his—then they would go home and finish this thing between them. She knew it, just as she knew the sun would rise tomorrow and another cow would get mastitis and Owen would ask her to sell the herd to him.

She also knew it was madness, but she wasn't sure she was strong enough to walk away. Her head lowered, just as he lifted his, and then something hot and wet slapped across her cheek and a paw landed in the back of her neck, shoving her face-down in the snow.

'Get off, dog,' Sam laughed, swiping Jess away, but the moment was gone. Jemima struggled to her feet, helped Sam out of the drift and banged the snow off his clothes while Jess bounced cheerfully round them barking and Noodle stood patiently waiting for someone to pick her up again.

They arrived back just as the grandfather clock in the parlour struck twelve. 'Come on, Cinderella, in you get,' Sam murmured, ushering her in with a firm hand against her waist. The kitchen was warm, and he set Noodle down on a chair by the Rayburn while Jemima lit the lantern and brushed the snow off her jeans.

She had put the kettle on and was just wondering whether or not he would kiss her goodnight and what would happen then, when there was a pounding on the door.

'Jemima? Where've you been? You all right?'

She would have been if she hadn't got the giggles.

She opened the door, took one look at Owen's scowling face and started to laugh.

'What's going on?' he muttered. 'You were out.'

'We've been to the Kings' for supper. We're fine, Owen.'

'Didn't know where you were. Anything could have happened.'

She suppressed a giggle. 'I didn't know I had to ask permission before I went out.'

'I was worried,' he went on doggedly. 'You don't have a lick of sense and he's just a city boy. You could have fallen in a drift.'

'Surely not.' She pulled the door open, squashing her smile. 'Come in, Owen. I've put the kettle on.'

'If you're sure. It's a strange time of night to go visiting—and how come you're back here?' he said, turning on Sam with a glower. 'Should have thought you'd stay with your folks, now the roads are clear and your fancy car's unstuck.'

Sam ignored the last part. 'Yes, it is a strange time to go visiting. What makes you think Jemima needs disturbing at this time of night? She might have been in bed.'

'That's what I was afraid of. Strikes me a chaperon might be in order,' Owen grumbled.

'I agree. The trouble is, who's chaperoning who, Owen?'

Jemima slapped the kettle back onto the hob and glared at them. 'Will you two both stop it? I don't need a chaperon—and I don't need you two squabbling over me! Sam's here to help with the water—'

'I could bring you water in a tank on the tractor—you know that. I did it for you in the summer when the pipe broke and I took it up the meadow to the beasts. You only have to ask.'

'She doesn't need you, Owen,' Sam cut in firmly.

Jemima, belatedly remembering the tank on Owen's tractor, wondered why Sam was turning down such a God-sent opportunity to escape.

'It would make things easier,' she said, feeling guilty for all the work Sam had done.

A second later she regretted her words. Owen's face looked smug, Sam looked like thunder and she wondered if she'd ever be able to understand men at all.

Owen got up. 'I'll see you in the morning, then—don't bother with the tea. I'm late to bed as it is. I suggest you get your sleep—unless you're going to let me take your herd up to ours for milking?'

'I don't need to; Sam fixed the little Lister engine,' she told him, and the scowl and smirk were reversed.

Men! She shooed Owen out, then had to deal with Sam.

'I was quite happy doing the water,' he began.

'I felt guilty. Owen can do it in no time.'

'I didn't mind,' he repeated stubbornly.

'Well, now you can go and stay with your grandparents—which is, after all, why you've come down here.'

He couldn't argue with her unassailable logic. Instead he went up to bed clutching a cup of tea, and that answered her question about whether he would kiss her goodnight.

Oh, well. It was probably just as well, anyway. Her life was complicated enough without having an affair with a man from the big smoke.

She wasn't sure what he did—an architect or surveyor or something? She remembered Mary mentioning it some time ago—he'd been nominated for an award for something. She ought to ask him—if he was still speaking to her.

It was by no means certain…

Sam was livid. He didn't hate people, as a rule, but he was working on changing that for the sake of Owen Stockdale.

First the snow shovel thingummybob, now a water tank, he thought disgustedly.

He stripped his clothes off, pulled on his pyjamas, hoisted the cat out of the way and crawled between the freezing sheets. If he didn't end up with frostbite it would be a living miracle.

He lay there, glaring at the ceiling and trying to work out why he was so angry with Owen, and why it mattered that he no longer had to spend back-breaking hours hauling water for Jemima. He hated doing it. Of all the things in the world that he could think of, it had to be right down there amongst eating raw fish and kissing frogs.

So why the heck he was so mad about having the job taken away from him, he couldn't imagine.

Except, of course, that it meant he had no excuse for hanging around with Jemima.

His mouth tightened and he drew in a breath and let it out on a heavy sigh. He didn't like the thought of Owen spending so much time with her, but she seemed convinced she was safe, and who was he to argue?

He hadn't seen the man for twenty-two years. Jemima was far better placed to judge him.

Dammit.

The cat purred and kneaded his chest through the sheet, and he let out a little yelp and removed its claws.

'You in league with that man?' he asked it accusingly, and the cat dribbled on his chest.

'Great. Marvellous. That's it.' He threw back the bedclothes, scooped the cat up and dumped it outside the door, just as Jemima was coming out of the bathroom.

'It dribbles,' he said economically.

She smiled and bent to pick it up, and the light from the lantern gleamed in her hair and turned her skin to gold. She looked like a cross between an angel and a pixie, her eyes sparkling with lively intelligence and her soft, kissable mouth curved in a smile.

And *that* was why he hated Owen Stockdale!

He was woken by the sound of Owen's tractor in the morning, bringing water to the cows in the barn. He peered out of the window and saw a big clear polythene tank in a metal frame attached to a hydraulic lift on the front of the tractor, and wondered how many buckets it would take to fill it.

Too many. Oh, well, he was free now. He could go and stay with his grandparents and mull over his future, which, after all, was why he was here.

He dropped the curtain back, pulled on his clothes and went down to the kitchen. The Rayburn needed rescuing again, and he got it going, put the kettle on and made a pot of tea, leaving it to brew until Owen left.

Petty, but probably the only way he could deal with it. Owen seemed to bring out the worst in him, provoking a childish jealousy he would have thought himself above.

Apparently he didn't know himself as well as he might.

He heard the tractor going, and took some tea out to Jemima.

'Saviour,' she said with a smile that would have lit beacons, and he forgot about the warm bed he'd abandoned and the sleep he could have been getting, and basked in the warmth of that glorious smile.

'You could have had a lie-in,' she reminded him, but he shook his head.

'Owen's tractor woke me. Anyway, I'm used to getting up early. I'm often on site by seven.'

She tipped her head and studied him. 'You're an architect, aren't you? Don't you work in London?'

He nodded. 'At the moment.'

A frown pleated her brow. 'At the moment?'

'I'm...' He hesitated, then sighed. 'Let's say I'm unsure about the future. I just know I won't carry on doing what I'm doing for the rest of my life. The line of work I'm in is very pressured—very make or break. I'm not sure there isn't more to life.'

She nodded thoughtfully. 'I know what you mean.'

He looked round. 'This place?'

'Here?' She laughed softly. 'I don't know about this. This is just a time out. I don't know what I'll do about it. No, I meant before. I was a solicitor, in London. Uncle Tom became ill and I chucked in my job and came down here to look after him while I thought about what I wanted to do.'

'And then he died and left it to you?'

She nodded. 'That's right. It seemed like a good idea at the time to keep it going, give me time to think. I may sell Owen the stock and live here and go back to work in Dorchester—do conveyancing or something. I don't know. I won't go back to what I was doing before.'

'Why did you give up? What was wrong with what you were doing?' he asked, curious about a tiny, feisty woman who'd thrown away everything to come and look after a dying uncle and had ended up scratching a pitiful living from his land.

'Oh—you know. I was doing matrimonial stuff—spoilt brats squabbling over their assets and fighting about who would have the children. It sickened me. So many of them seemed to have such petty reasons for splitting up, as if they didn't have a real foundation for their marriage in the first place.'

'Maybe they didn't.'

She shrugged. 'Maybe not. They shouldn't have got married then, should they?'

She perched on an upturned bucket and waved a hand at a bale of straw. He sat on it, nursing his tea while he leant against the wall and watched the cows. One of them climbed up on the back of another, and he raised a brow and turned to her.

'Is that a bull?'

She shook her head, laughing. 'No. She's in season. I need to call the AI man. A couple of them are ready.'

'Ready?' he asked, not sure what was coming and not sure he really wanted to know.

'Fertile. The man from the AI centre—'

'AI?'

'Artificial insemination. They bring a little straw of frozen semen and—'

He threw up his hands, laughing. 'OK, OK, I get the drift! So, they're in the mood, are they?'

She grinned and nodded. 'That's right. I meant to ring him on Friday but there didn't seem a lot of point with the weather forecast. Owen tells me the road's clear now, so I should be all right for tomorrow.'

She handed him her mug and stood up. 'Back to work. The engine's wonderful—thank you for fixing it.'

He straightened up, towering over her and wondering

how she could be so small and yet so tough. 'My pleasure. When will you be finished?'

'When I've mucked out. I have to keep them in because of the snow and it takes longer working round them.'

He felt a rash moment coming on, but couldn't stop it. 'Want me to start for you?'

'Would you?' Her face lit up, and he gave a hollow laugh.

'I can hardly wait.'

'You don't have to.'

'I know.'

Their eyes met and locked, and she smiled again, the smile that set him alight inside and turned his resolve to mush.

'Thanks,' she murmured, and he knew to his disgust that he would have done anything for her.

He worked like a demon. She finished the milking, pouring the milk away and mourning the waste, but until the power was back there was nothing else she could do with it. He was still forking away, whistling softly, humming every now and again, and if she hadn't known better she'd have thought he was enjoying himself.

She wondered why he hadn't ever got married. Goodness knows he was good-looking enough, and apart from a regrettable tendency to brawl with the competition he would make someone a good husband one day, she thought.

Not her, though. Apart from the fact that she was simply too busy to get involved with anyone, her work had scared her off marriage. So many people with shattered dreams, so many broken promises, so much wasted sorrow.

No, it was easier to avoid it.

She went over to him and removed the fork from his hand. 'I can manage now,' she said, and he stepped back with a puzzled frown.

'I can finish.'

'It's OK. Really. Why don't you pack up your stuff and go on over to your grandparents? They'll be thrilled to have you.'

He took the fork out of her hand and hefted it, looking at her searchingly.

'Did I do something wrong?' he asked softly, and she had a stupid, stupid urge to put her head on his shoulder and cry her eyes out.

'No. It's nothing to do with you.'

'Owen?'

'No, not Owen either. Nothing. Just go. I can manage, really.'

He nodded and went, putting the fork down by the door as he left the barn, and she watched him walk across the yard, Jess at his heels, and into the kitchen.

Damn. Still, she was better off without him. It was less complicated that way…

CHAPTER FIVE

SHE missed him.

It was ridiculous, really, because she'd spent a year managing on her own and he'd only been around for a couple of days, not even that. Still, she missed him. She missed his laugh, his company—even his irritating whistling.

And she missed his protection when Owen came round later that afternoon with the tractor to do the water again and cornered her in the barn with the young stock.

Not that he did anything.

He just stood there, very big and very close, and asked if Sam had gone.

'Yes—he's gone over to his grandparents,' she told him, and was irritated by the glint of amusement and victory in his eyes.

'Didn't need him around here anyway,' Owen said, and there was something very possessive and proprietorial about the way he said it that irritated her.

'Actually, I did need him,' she corrected softly. 'He was very helpful over the water.'

'You should have asked,' Owen told her again. 'You know I would have done it. I'd do anything for you.'

She looked up into his big brown eyes and remembered Sam calling him Owen the Ox.

How appropriate. Big, lumbering, loyal and totally insensitive.

'I know you would,' she said, stifling a sigh. 'Thank

you. I'm very grateful for your help—it's reassuring to have good neighbours.'

'I'm more than just a neighbour,' he pointed out.

'A friend, then,' she amended hastily, before he could say any more. 'And as I say, I'm very grateful, but I must get on; I've still got to feed the hens and pick up the eggs.'

'I could give you a hand.'

'Owen, it's OK. You've done more than enough. I can manage now.'

He grunted, but he went, leaving her sighing with relief. She sagged back against the wall of the barn and listened to the tractor going, then shut the calves up, picked up the lantern and went into the hen house.

It was thawing, she realised. With the characteristic fickleness of early spring, the weather had changed from blizzard to balmy in just forty-eight hours, and now the heaped-up snow was wilting, growing heavy and plopping off the branches like ripe fruit. She listened to the steady drip of the trees and the rush of the stream, and felt relief.

If necessary, once it was thawed she could turn the milkers out into the paddock by the stream and they could drink their fill without anyone having to carry it, so she wouldn't have to be beholden to any of these men.

She put the hens to bed, went in and let the dogs out for a run. The snow was too deep for Noodle to be out all day, and Jess had had a good run this morning, so she'd shut her up as well. Now she found herself heading up the hill towards Dick and Mary—and Sam—and had to stop herself. Stupid. Stupid, stupid, stupid. Leave him alone.

She missed him. She took the dogs a different way,

and she remembered last night, when they'd all gone out together to his grandparents, and what fun it had been.

He'd fallen in the snow drift, and if Owen hadn't come round—

Crazy. She mustn't start thinking like that.

The dogs followed her back into the kitchen, and she missed his big body clogging up the space. The chair that had always been Uncle Tom's had become Sam's in the space of a weekend, and now sat tormenting her by the fire like a pregnant pause.

She fed the dogs, just because she had to do something, and then she made scrambled eggs and overcooked them, so they weren't like the ones Sam had done—

'This is ridiculous! You've got to stop,' she chastised herself, but it was hard with nothing to fill the gap.

She went upstairs and stripped his bed, throwing the sheets in the corner of the bathroom until the power was back on and she could use the washing machine again. They smelt faintly of him, and she had to force herself not to pick them up again and sniff them.

Ridiculous. She really ought to get out more. She was losing it, seriously losing it, bottled up here all on her own with nothing but the animals for company.

There was always Owen, of course!

She went back down to the kitchen, put the kettle on and twiddled the radio. The batteries were getting low and it was crackling furiously, so in the end she turned it off and sat listening to Noodle snoring.

And then, through the silence of the evening, she heard a siren, and blue flashing lights went past on a large vehicle. A fire engine?

The siren stopped, and she tugged on her coat and

boots and went out into the yard, concerned. It sounded as if it had stopped at the Stockdales' farm—

It had. A fire engine stood in the lane, lights flashing, but there was no sign of fire. No sign of anything, but she could hear shouting. She ran down the lane, her heart thumping, and as she squeezed past the fire engine she saw Owen's tractor lying on its roof in the ditch by the yard entrance.

'Owen?' she whispered, and a man appeared at her side.

'Can I help you, miss?'

She looked up at him. 'Is anyone in the cab?'

'Farmer's son—who are you?'

'A neighbour—is he hurt?'

'Don't know yet. He's talking. Parents are over there. Perhaps you'd like to join them.'

She went over to the group huddled around the cab, and saw Mrs Stockdale struggling with tears.

'I'm all right, Mother, it's just my arm,' Owen was saying. He sounded a little strained but otherwise normal, and she peered in. He was lying on his side, one arm trapped awkwardly beneath him, and there was a fireman talking to him through the shattered windscreen.

He saw her and smiled bravely. 'Jemima—look after my mother, would you? Tell her I'm all right. Take her inside or something.'

'I'm not leaving his side,' his mother said firmly. 'I know I can't do a lot, but I can be here.'

His father said nothing, just stood there watching the winch on the fire engine being attached to the tractor to try and tug it back on its wheels.

It took ages, and once it slipped and Owen bellowed with pain, but then it was up enough to prop the far side and they were able to get him out.

'Broken arm,' the fireman told the paramedic who had since arrived, and Owen was borne off in the ambulance, looking pale and shaken. He was accompanied by his equally pale and shaken mother, and his father followed in the car.

'Any idea where we should put the tractor?' the fireman asked Jemima once it was upright.

She shrugged. 'I'll park it in the yard. I expect it's still driveable.'

The fireman looked her up and down. 'You got a licence?' he asked sceptically.

She rolled her eyes and ignored him, climbing into the battered cab and avoiding the broken glass that littered the floor and seat. It started, but when she drove it forwards the steering was extremely weird. Still, it limped onto the yard and she parked it more or less up against the barn. It would have to do.

She pulled the keys out and put them through the letter box—not that she thought anyone would be likely to steal it, but you never could tell—and then she went home. It was midnight, and it was beginning to dawn on her that for all she might not have wanted him, she'd just lost Owen and his water-carrier.

Which meant, if the power didn't come back on by morning, she'd have to carry water alone…

'Hi, there.'

She looked up from Betsy's side and saw Sam outlined in the barn door, backlit by the early-morning sun. He was wearing a suit, looking clean and tidy and very much the city gent, and she was more than ever conscious of her bedraggled hair and chapped, cracked hands and the streak of whatever on her cheek.

She stood up and went over to him so he didn't have

to come into the barn in his beautifully polished shoes. 'Hi, yourself. You look dressed for work.'

He grinned ruefully. 'I am. I'm just on my way back. I thought I'd call in and say goodbye.'

She ought just to say goodbye back and let him go. She didn't have time to stop—

'Cup of tea?'

'Have you got time?'

She smiled. 'I can make time.'

They went into the kitchen to be greeted ecstatically by the dogs. Sam was, anyway. They just wagged at her and grinned. Sam was the special person.

She knew just how they felt. If it wasn't so disgraceful she'd roll over on her back and wiggle so he'd tickle *her* tummy—

The phone rang in the nick of time, and she went into the parlour and picked it up. It was Mrs Stockdale, ringing to say that Owen was home and had his arm in plaster, and to thank her for putting the tractor out of the way and dealing with the men.

'My pleasure. Give him my best wishes and tell him I hope he's soon more comfortable,' she said, hoping he wouldn't misconstrue her neighbourly concern, and went back to Sam.

'Owen's mother—he's out of hospital now.'

'Hospital?'

She shook her head. 'Of course, you don't know. His tractor turned over last night in the ditch and he broke his arm. It's quite tricky to see there by the gate, and with the snow I suppose he just misjudged it—'

'So who's doing the water?'

She shrugged, and his eyes narrowed.

'Jemima, you can't manage on your own.'

'I shall have to. You're going back to work—and anyway, it won't be for long. Now it's Monday they'll get the power sorted out—'

'They've been working on it all weekend. There's no telling how long it could take. What if it's three days?'

Her shoulders sagged with despair before she could stop them, and Sam shook his head, pushed past her and went out.

'Sam?' She followed him, stomping into her boots and tugging on her coat as she went up the yard. 'Sam, wait! What's wrong?'

'You're an idiot is what's wrong!' he yelled over his shoulder. 'A stubborn, foolhardy, independent little streak of nonsense with sawdust for brains.'

She stopped dead, hands on her hips. 'Well, thanks a bunch!' she yelled after him. 'It's nice to know who your friends are in a crisis! I'm glad you're going. You've done nothing but criticise—'

He opened the door of his car, pulled out the leather sports bag and slammed the door.

Her jaw sagged, and he flipped her mouth shut with his finger as he came back past.

She spun on her heel and ran after him. 'Sam? What are you doing?'

He shouldered open the kitchen door and headed for the stairs, ripping off his tie as he went. 'I'm helping you, you little idiot! What the hell do you think I'm doing?'

'Well, maybe I don't need your help!' she yelled up the stairs after him. 'Maybe I can manage without you, you bossy, autocratic, jumped-up little city boy!'

There was an ominous silence, then he appeared in view, dressed only in a shirt undone all down the front, a pair of skimpy briefs and his socks, and sat down on the top step.

'Do you want me to go?' he said softly.

Her shoulders drooped. 'No,' she croaked, her throat betraying her, raw with emotion and all the yelling. 'No, of course I don't want you to go.'

'Well, then, make the tea, and I'll be down in a minute.'

He stood up and turned round, and she watched him go and wondered how she'd ever thought his body was soft. He was solid muscle, sleek and sinuous and graceful, with a soft scattering of hair over his chest and down those long, powerful legs.

It made her ache with longing.

She went back into the kitchen, poured out some breakfast cereal and munched it while she waited for him. He wasn't long. He'd put on his jeans and a thick rugby shirt, and she busied herself pouring the tea so she didn't pour herself into his arms.

'Here,' she said, feeling small and ungracious and confused, and he took the tea out of her hand, put it down and hugged her.

'I would have coped,' she mumbled into his shoulder, and he squeezed her.

'I know. Maybe I want to be here. Maybe I don't want to go back to my job and I was just looking for an excuse to escape.'

She tipped back her head and looked up at him. 'Really?'

His grin was boyish and mischievous and a little wry. 'Don't you worry about my motives. I'll deal with them.'

She smiled, and he patted her shoulder and let her go, to her disappointment. She rather liked being held by him.

He picked up his tea and sat down in his chair, shoving Noodle off onto the floor, and stretched out his legs with a sigh. 'So, Owen's broken his arm, eh?'

Was that a smirk? She eyed him thoughtfully. It looked suspiciously like it.

'Yes, he has, and it's a disaster for them. He could be out of action for weeks and his father hasn't been well,' she said accusingly.

He arched a brow. 'You're very defensive all of a sudden.'

'You were smirking.'

'I was not.'

'You looked pleased.'

He met her eyes. 'Maybe I'm pleased that I've got a genuine excuse to spend more time with you.'

His honesty stopped her in her tracks. She swallowed. 'Why would you want to spend time with me?'

He laughed. 'Because for some reason I can't quite fathom, I like you, you aggravating little wench.'

'Oh.' She coloured, a warm glow suffusing her cheeks as she digested his words. She didn't know what else to say, so she buried her nose in her mug and hid the smile of pleasure that wouldn't go away. He liked her!

She quite forgot that she didn't want him to. Somehow it didn't seem to matter any more…

He worked like a demon, striding up and down the yard along the path of ash they'd laid, carrying bucket after bucket without a murmur. Then he mucked out, barrowing the soiled straw away to the muck trailer and piling it in until it was full.

He paused with a full barrow behind Daisy, whose udder Jemima was gently massaging. 'The trailer's full. Where shall I put it now?'

She opened her mouth to reply, just as Daisy's tail

lifted. The warning was on the tip of her tongue when Daisy coughed, and a vile green jetstream hit Sam right in the chest.

He yelled and leapt back, plucking fruitlessly at the rugby shirt, and an expression of horrified incredulity spread over his face. 'Ah, no, it's inside my shirt!'

She tried. She really did try not to laugh, but it was too much. She doubled over, clutching her sides and wheezing while Sam spluttered and stamped round and brought down curses on the heads of all the cattle.

Finally he ground to a halt and she looked up, wiping the tears from her eyes. 'You'd better go and change,' she suggested, trying desperately to subdue her mirth.

'Into what? This is my last shirt—apart from my work shirts, and I'm not using them. No, if I change another one of them will take up the challenge. I might as well finish off first.'

'Are you sure?'

He nodded tersely, and her respect for him edged up another notch. Wow. 'So, where do I put the straw I'm taking out?' he asked again, strategically placing himself in the centre of the barn, away from all the tails.

'Oh—round the corner. I'll show you. Are you sure you want to go on?'

He shot her a fulminating glance, grabbed the barrow and followed her in grim-lipped silence.

'Here, please,' she told him, pointing at a steaming heap from which the snow had cleared. 'When it's rotted down I sell it.'

'Smells pretty rotten already from where I'm standing,' he grumbled, and she looked at the evil spreading stain on his shirt-front and had to stifle another smile.

'I'm sorry. There wasn't time to warn you. It was just because she coughed—'

'I did notice,' he said drily, and began forking muck like a madman.

To get away? To finish and get changed? Or just to burn off frustration? Who could tell?

Sam was not in the best of moods. His nose was immediately above what had to be probably his least favourite smell in the world right now, and he had another problem. As the vile goop dried, it stuck all the hairs on his chest together, so that every swing of his arms or movement of his shoulders pulled the hairs out.

He'd heard of women having their legs waxed, and even swimmers having their chests done, but it was only now that he began to get an inkling of what that might involve.

He was suddenly very glad that he wasn't either a woman or a swimmer!

'Sam, could you get that down for me, please?' Jemima asked, pointing to a high shelf in the back of the barn. 'The old one's run out.'

There was a big pot of something called Stockholm Tar, and the way his luck was going he thought it quite likely he would tip it on his head. He reached up carefully, and let out a little yelp.

'Sam?'

'It's all right,' he growled, and winced again.

'What's wrong? Are you hurt?'

He looked down into her upturned face, filled with concern, and closed his eyes. He didn't want to see her laugh.

'My chest hairs are all stuck together. When I stretch, they pull. They pull out. It hurts.'

He didn't see her laugh, but he heard her—well, a

quickly stifled snigger, anyway. His eyes flew open. 'Do you want this or not?' he growled.

'Yes, please—if you can manage it without doing yourself an injury.'

'You just want to see me suffer,' he muttered, and, pulling his lips into a tight line to stop the protest escaping, he reached up, grabbed the pot and handed it to her.

'So brave,' she murmured, fluttering her lashes, and he had a crazy urge to dump her in the water trough. Instead he dusted off his hands, went back to his barrow and carefully and gingerly finished off the mucking out.

She came to help him, and the moment it was finished she turned to him and grinned. 'Right, let's go and see how bald you are.'

'Sadist,' he growled at her, and followed her into the kitchen.

'Take off the shirt.'

'You are kidding. It's stuck to me.'

She studied him from all sides, then nodded. 'You're right. We'll wet you.' And without any further ado, she grabbed a cloth, dipped it in the cold water in the sink and started dolloping it all over him.

'Could we do this with warm water?' he said through clenched teeth, and she relented and poured the kettle into the bowl. It was too hot, then, of course, but he wasn't going to say another word. Instead he stood there in grim-lipped silence while she peeled the shirt away from his body inch by inch, and then finally he was able to pull it over his head.

'I'll wash it,' she offered, and he dropped the soggy article into her outstretched hand and looked down at his chest.

'I think I need a wash,' he said drily.

'Mmm. Perhaps a visit to your grandparents?'

'Good idea. Want another bath?'

'I'd love another bath.'

'Let's go for lunch.'

She grinned. 'What a good idea. Mary always makes the most wonderful soup.' She paused. 'I think we ought to clean you up a bit more, though, first. Here, you do the front; I'll do the sides where you can't see.'

It seemed like a good idea, before he put anything else on, and by the time they'd finished he felt a little more human.

'You've got some on your neck, still,' she murmured, and went up on tiptoe to dab just under his chin. Then she dropped back down and ran her hands down his chest, settling them on his waist like sandpaper.

'Your hands aren't much softer yet,' he said wryly. 'I think I'd better give them some more attention—it's like being touched up by a builder!'

She dropped her hands and stepped back, laughing. 'How on earth would you know about that?' she chuckled, and he laughed and pulled her back.

'Wouldn't you like to know?' he murmured.

He saw the change in her eyes, saw the softening, the warmth as her arms slid round him and her hands laid against his back, saw the invitation in her eyes and on her lips, and just as his head came down there was a pounding on the door.

'If that's Owen, I'll kill him,' he vowed softly.

She eased away, shushed the dogs and opened the door.

'Hello, Owen. We were just talking about you. How are you?' she said, and her voice was gentle with concern.

Sam stifled his annoyance and his animosity. The man

was hurt, and he had been a good neighbour to Jemima. There was no need to be rude—but on the other hand, he might as well know where he stood...

He stationed himself behind Jemima, hands curled proprietorially round her shoulders, and smiled a greeting. 'Hi, Owen. Sorry to hear about your arm. How is it?'

Owen's eyes tracked over his naked chest in disbelief. 'It'll do. I'm sorry, I didn't mean to interrupt anything.' His mouth tight, he turned on his heel and was going when Jemima reached out and put a hand on his shoulder.

'Owen, stay. You aren't interrupting anything. Have a cup of tea.'

He shook his head. 'No, I can see you're busy. I'll go on. I just wanted to make sure you were all right, but I can see you are.'

'He was just changing—'

'Thanks for your help last night. Call if you need anything.'

And he went, striding down the path, pride holding his shoulders square. Sam actually felt sorry for him, and it must have showed, because Jemima turned round and looked up at him and did a mild double take. 'What, not gloating, Sam?' she murmured.

'Doesn't seem kind. After all, it could just as easily have been me in my car turning over the other day.' And anyway, he could have added, it's me that's here with you, me that nearly kissed you.

Me that's walking you home later.

CHAPTER SIX

'SO, WHAT'S this award you've been nominated for?'

Sam shoved his hands in his pockets and scuffed the snow, warm colour flooding his neck. 'How did you find out about that?'

Jemima stopped walking and turned towards him. He looked embarrassed and very human, and she realised just how modest he was about his apparently considerable talent. 'Mary mentioned something a while ago. She's very proud of you.'

He grinned wryly. 'Evidently.'

'Well?' she prompted, when it was obvious he wasn't going to elaborate.

'It's a design award, that's all. I may not even get it. She's jumping the gun.'

Jemima checked for the dogs and called them, watching as Jess streaked back across the snow towards her. 'Nevertheless, whatever you did must be pretty good to get nominated. What did you design?'

He kicked the snow, sending wet blobs of it flying. 'Oh, it's an old maltings on the South Bank. It's stood idle for years, and the local council wanted something done to it. I followed their brief, really.'

And there was so much more he wasn't saying, Jemima knew. She prodded further as they walked home, but he wouldn't give a lot, only that in addition to council offices there was a theatre and a craft centre and community hall, conference facilities, sheltered housing, a restaurant, art gallery and so on.

'And you designed it all?' she said, stunned.

'Not all, and not without help, but I oversaw it all, yes.'

'Wow,' she breathed, impressed. 'That must have been some undertaking.'

He shrugged. 'Pretty time-consuming, but at least I didn't have to commute. I live there. It seemed the easiest way to make sure I was available at all times, and they wanted some private flats to sell off to cover some of the cost, so it suited us all, really. The flats were the first part of it to be completed.'

'Is it a nice place to live?' she asked, wondering now about the man who'd been carrying water for her for days, the man who'd grown from the child she'd befriended briefly all those years ago.

He looked around, his eyes narrowing against the glare of the sun, and gave a rueful smile. 'Not in the way that this is, but I suppose it's all right. My flat itself is lovely—it's on the top floor and so I've got the roof beams. Being a maltings it's all a bit open and vaulted, which is great in the summer but a bit odd in the winter.'

'Cold, I should think. High ceilings usually are.'

He laughed. 'These ceilings are nearly twenty foot high—more in places. There are fans in the roof to blow the heat back down, and I've got a very efficient heating system to compensate, but it's a very interesting old complex. It was fun doing it, and the flats have sold like hot cakes. It's on the Thames, which is a plus, of course. The boats are interesting to watch, but some parts of the area are a bit hit and miss just there. It has its moments, I suppose.'

She tried to picture it, but failed. 'I'd love to see it.'

'You should come up.'

'And leave the animals?' she said wryly, wishing she could.

'I've got pictures—I'll send them to you.'

'Thanks.'

She stared down at the ground, noting absently that they were walking in step, and wished the power would never come back on and whisk him off to his world. It sounded busy and high-powered and a little daunting.

They arrived back at her little cottage and she tried to see it with his eyes. Not a smart move. She looked at the sagging gutter, the rotten window-frame in the bathroom, the green bits round the bottom where the rising damp was eating at the brickwork, and she imagined his bright, vaulted, newly finished flat with its hugely high ceilings.

Not a flattering comparison.

They went inside, dumped the bags with their wash things and fed the dogs, then went over to the barn to start the evening milking and water fetching.

She thought about his world—the world she'd left, the world of money and success and divorce and bitterness and acrimony—and wondered what he really thought of her and her little farm.

Unbelievably provincial.

Oh, well. She cranked the handle on the little Lister engine, topped up the water in the reservoir and went to milk her cows. Once the milk cooler was back on the tanker would come to her again, but in the meantime she was pouring the milk that the calves didn't need onto the muck heap, and every day that passed left her poorer.

She tried not to think of her overdraft, of the state of her car and the stupidly damaged tractor, but in between cows there was nothing else to do. Sam was striding back and forth with buckets, and she watched him and wished their worlds weren't so hopelessly far apart, not only in terms of distance but also in lifestyle.

She could always go back to his world, of course. There was nothing but stubborn loyalty tying her to Uncle Tom's farm, and he'd never have expected her to do what she was doing. Still, the very thought—

The little engine coughed, and the revs dropped a touch before picking up. She put the cluster on the last cow, emptied the milk out and went to see what Sam was up to.

'Nearly done?' he asked her, still able to find a smile despite the sheen of sweat on his brow and the endless load he'd shifted.

'On the last cow now. The Lister engine's sounding a bit funny—do you think you could have a look at it?'

He grinned. 'Sure—if you finish off the water to the calves.'

'Oh, I suppose I could—you drive a hard bargain,' she said with a smile, and he tapped her nose with the tip of his finger in a silly, tender gesture that left her knees weak and made her wish she could keep him here for ever.

It was dusk, and the snow was melting fast now. She walked down to the stream with the buckets, listening to the trickling of water under the snow all around her. The stream was up, full of melt-water, and she knew it would be days before she could turn the cattle out.

Oh, well.

She dipped the first bucket and set it down, then turned for the second.

As she did she caught sight of a fox, slinking along on the other bank, heading for her hen house.

'Hey, you, go away! Leave my hens alone!' she shouted.

Startled, it lifted its head and met her eyes, then vanished into the dusk. She shook her head. It was hungry, poor thing. It might have young to feed, but that was no excuse to steal her chickens.

She turned for the second bucket, not concentrating, and stepped off the cinder path onto the slush. It disappeared beneath her, and to her horror she felt herself slide down the bank and into the water.

'Sam!' she yelled, just as she hit the water and felt the icy cold shock of it on her legs. She screamed, flailing to keep her balance, but the current was too strong and her legs were tugged out from under her.

She reached out as she toppled and grabbed the edge of the step, her fingers fastening on the rough stone like limpets.

She tried to scream again, but the cold had robbed her lungs of air and all she could feel was terror and the greedy fingers of the water, dragging her down...

'Jem?'

Sam cut the engine and listened, but there was nothing. He was sure he'd heard her—

'Jem?' He straightened and went out to the yard, calling her, but there was no reply. Had she gone inside?

It seemed unlikely. There was no light in the kitchen, and he could hear the dogs barking.

Odd.

He went into the other barn, to the youngsters, but there was no sign of her, so he went down to the stream. There was no sign of her there, either, but the buckets were there. Whatever was she up to? He called again, and tipped his head on one side.

Had that been her? A tiny sound, more of a wail than a shout, coming from—

'Oh, lord,' he murmured, and broke into a run, skidding to a halt by the side of the stream.

Her fingers were clamped on the step, blue with cold, locked onto it so tight he could hardly free them, and her body was lying horizontally in the water, waving in the current like a reed.

Fear gripped him, and, kneeling down, he reached in for her.

'I've got you,' he yelled, grabbing her by the back of the neck and hoisting her out of the rushing stream.

She sagged against his chest, icy water streaming off her and soaking him, making him gasp with the shock of the cold. 'Sam?' she whispered soundlessly.

His hands tightened convulsively. 'Oh, Jemima, what the hell were you doing? You could have been killed!'

'Fell,' she mouthed.

She shuddered feebly, shocked and frozen, and he hauled her up into his arms and staggered to his feet. 'I've got to get you warm,' he told her grimly. 'Just hang on.'

He carried her into the kitchen, dumped her on a chair by the Rayburn and shut the dogs in the parlour out of the way. Then he ripped off his coat, pushed up his sleeves and set about stripping her out of her sodden clothes.

She was blue with cold—literally blue, all over. He grabbed a towel off the front of the Rayburn and wrapped it round her, tugging her to her feet so he could pull down her clinging jeans and let the warmth to her legs.

'C-c-c-o-old,' she juddered, shaking convulsively, and he ran upstairs, grabbed the quilt off her bed and some towels from the bathroom and ran down again.

He didn't know the first thing about hypothermia, but

he knew one thing. She had to get warm, slowly and thoroughly, and the best way to do that was to get dry. So he rubbed her arms and legs with the towels, chafing the blue skin and scrubbing at the goosebumps while she sat huddled in the quilt.

Her lips were blue, her face was chalk white and he felt sick. 'I'm going to call an ambulance.'

'No—I'm all right,' she said shakily. 'Just—hold me.'

He hesitated for a moment, then ripped his sweater over his head, shucked off his jeans and picked her up, spreading the quilt on the floor in front of the fire. Then he lay down, pulled her into the curve of his body and threw the quilt over them both.

She was like ice. Her flesh was stiff with cold, her back freezing against his naked chest, and he sucked his breath in and held her firmly back against his warmth. She moaned softly, wriggling harder against him, and he wrapped her feet in his and laid his hands over the soft curve of her abdomen and waited for the shaking to stop.

Finally, after an age, she seemed to relax, just the odd shudder racking her slender frame from time to time, and he reached out and grabbed a cushion off the chair, tucking it under her head to make her more comfortable.

'Don't go,' she whispered.

'I'm not going.'

She slumped against him again, sighing with relief, and he let his hands relax. The arm underneath her was going to sleep, so he shifted it slightly, bending his elbow so he could stroke her hair. The other hand wrapped around hers, the fingers meshing, holding her safe.

He might have lost her. If he hadn't heard her, if he'd been just a few more moments—

It was a sickening thought, and his fingers tightened convulsively.

'Sam?'

'It's OK. Are you all right?'

'Mmm. Sleepy.'

'Go to sleep, then. I'll look after you.'

She did, almost immediately, her breathing steadying and becoming shallow and even, her limbs soft and warm now, relaxed against his. He closed his eyes, let the tension drain away and rested his head against hers. Just a few minutes, he promised himself. Just a little longer...

She woke up feeling hot. There was something scorching all the way down her back, from her neck to her ankles, and something else hot and heavy curled around her breast.

Sam's hand, and Sam behind her, warming her.

She would have died without him, she realised, and a shudder ran through her at the thought. She shifted slightly and his hand tightened, the fingers curving reflexively to cup her breast. She eased his hand away, regretting the loss of contact, and tried to wriggle away, but he pulled his hand free and wrapped it round her, pulling her back.

'Where are you going?' he mumbled.

'Nowhere. It's dark. Where are the dogs?'

'Next door. They're OK.'

'They need to go out. I can hear them.'

'I'll do it. Are you OK?'

She laid a hand against his, curled possessively around her ribs this time. 'I'm fine. Thanks, Sam. You saved my life—'

'Don't.' His arm tightened convulsively. 'If I'd finished off first before I went to look at the engine it would never have happened.'

'Don't be silly. You were on your way to London. It's just lucky you were here.'

They were silent for a moment, both dwelling on what might have happened if he'd gone back as he'd intended.

'I'm all right,' she said softly, and turned towards him. 'Don't torture yourself.'

He pulled her into his arms, burying his head in the hollow of her shoulder, and she hugged him briefly, then eased away. 'Sam, the dogs—'

'OK.' He crawled out of their makeshift bed and tucked the quilt back round her, then after lighting the lantern he tugged on his damp jeans and sweater, put the dogs out, made a cup of tea and put the Rayburn to bed for the night.

The dogs came in, wet-pawed and enthusiastic, greeting Jemima lovingly. She hugged them, sitting up against the wall, the quilt anchored firmly under her arms, and Sam handed her a cup of tea and perched on the edge of a chair, watching her grimly over the rim of his mug.

'I'm fine, Sam. Stop worrying.'

'You were blue. Blue all over—blue and orange. Just another few moments in that water—'

'Sam, stop it!'

He shut his eyes, his head bowed, and he took a long, deep breath. Poor Sam. She could hardly remember anything about it—just seeing the fox and slipping, and then the terrible, numbing cold until she woke naked in his arms. It must have been far worse for him.

She pushed the dogs off and put her tea down, then wriggled over to him, still wrapped in the quilt. 'Sam?' she murmured.

He lifted his head and his eyes opened, vague and

unfocused, still seeing her in the river, she imagined. She laid a hand on his. 'Sam, come to bed with me.'

They focused then, spearing her like blue lasers. For an age he was silent, and she thought she'd misunderstood all that he'd said, all the subtle looks and signals, the laughter they'd shared.

And then he stood and drew her to her feet, and scooped her into his arms. 'Bring the lantern,' he said tersely, and she hooked it up with her fingers and dangled it out to the side while he manoeuvred them through the doorway and up the stairs to her room.

He set her down carefully on the edge of the bed, then took the lantern from her hand and put it on the chest of drawers. The cat followed them in, and he turned and scooped it up and put it firmly back on the landing, then closed the door.

Jemima sat on the bed, snuggled in the quilt, and watched breathlessly as he reached over his head and grasped the neck of his sweater, tugging it off. His skin gleamed in the lamplight, gliding smoothly over the underlying muscles, making her fingers ache to touch him.

He dropped the sweater on the floor, then reached for his jeans. The rasp of his zip made her breath catch in her throat, and she waited, mesmerised, as he hooked his thumbs in the waistband and peeled off jeans and briefs in one swift, economical movement.

He came to her then, a vulnerable uncertainty touching the depths of his eyes. There was no uncertainty in hers, in any part of her. She wanted him as much as he wanted her.

She stood up, leaving the quilt behind, and reached out for him. His lips met hers as their bodies closed the gap, and she laid her hands against the strong column of his spine and wished she could stroke him, touch him as she wanted to, but her hands were so harsh, so rough and coarse with work that she was ashamed.

'Jem?'

He must have sensed her hesitation. She looked up into his eyes and ached with longing and misery. 'I want to touch you.'

'So touch me.'

'You said it was like being touched up by a builder—'

He made a soft growl in the back of his throat. 'Touch me, Jem,' he whispered, and his voice was ragged with need. 'Please, sweetheart, touch me…'

So she did, letting her fingers explore the contours of his back, his shoulders, his ribs, and all the while his hands echoed hers, like a dance.

She realised he was following her, so she let her hands slide up his ribs, so that her palms covered the taut, pebbled coins of his nipples, and felt his hands close possessively over her breasts.

It robbed her of air, driving the last of her breath out in a shaken sigh. 'Sam?'

'I need you, Jem,' he muttered, and she could feel the tension in him, in the rigid cords of muscle under her hands, in the jerky movement of his chest as he breathed, in the savage pounding of his heart against her palm.

She drew back and turned, picking the quilt up and throwing it across the bed, then flicking it aside before turning back to him.

'Coming?' she asked.

He laughed softly. 'I hope not—not yet.'

Their eyes locked, and she held out her hand. 'Come to me, Sam,' she murmured. 'I need you, too.'

The sheets were freezing against her bare skin, and she shivered slightly as she lay back and waited for him. She didn't have long to wait. He was there, his arms circling her, lifting her against him, his mouth locking on hers with desperation.

Good heavens, she thought, no one's ever really kissed me before, and then she stopped thinking and gave herself up to sensation...

Sam lay listening to the soft, even sound of her breathing, his arms cradling her against his body. She was draped across him bonelessly, her hair tangling in his mouth, her slender limbs sprawled in utter relaxation.

He was stunned by how he felt. It was as if there'd never been anyone else, as if the handful of carefully chosen and cherished women who'd gone before were no longer there. He couldn't imagine touching anyone else the way he'd touched Jemima—couldn't imagine anyone else touching him with the tentative, hesitant strokes she'd used to drive him wild.

Emotion rose to choke him, filling his chest until there wasn't room for air. He let his breath out in what sounded suspiciously like a sob, and squeezed his eyes tight against the hot sting of tears.

She could have died tonight, he thought. If her fingers had slipped and she'd been carried downstream—if he hadn't heard her call, or heard the dogs bark—she could be lying on a slab now, waiting for a pathologist to come and—

He dragged in a huge breath and hugged her closer. She made a warm, sleepy noise and snuggled against him, and he tipped her head and kissed her awake.

'Sam?' she murmured sleepily, and her arms slid up and circled his neck, drawing him down to her.

He went willingly, his body claiming hers again, rising to new heights in her arms as he lost himself in the tenderness of her embrace.

* * *

Jemima woke to sunlight filtering through the curtains, and the sound of running water in the loft. She lay, replete and contented, trying to analyse the sound and what was strange about it, but she was too busy letting her hands walk over Sam, stroking the heavy length of thigh that had fastened over her legs, pinning them down.

She ran a finger behind his knee and he twitched, ticklish there even in his sleep. She smiled lazily and laid her hand against the corded muscle of his thigh, just enjoying the feel of him for the few precious minutes that were left to them.

They would have to get up soon and see to the stock. The calves hadn't finished getting their water last night, thanks to her unscheduled dip, and they would have to do that first—

'Of course!' she said, sitting bolt upright. Sam's arm fell off her chest and slid down to her thighs, and he woke and blinked at her.

'Jemima? What's going on?'

'The power's back on!' she said excitedly, turning to him and grabbing him by the hand. 'The pump's working, filling the tank! Sam, it's all right now! We won't have to carry water any more.'

And there would be no need for him to stay. Her face must have fallen, because he reached up and drew her down, shifting so that he lay over her. His lips met hers, seeking tenderly, and with the knowledge of him leaving she gave him everything she was, everything she could be.

He was more demanding than before, his hands a little rougher, touched with desperation as he took her over the edge with him one last glorious time.

There was no sleepy aftermath. He rolled away from

her in silence, tugged on his clothes and went down to the kitchen. She heard him putting the dogs out and going out into the yard, checking the water, presumably.

She felt—not used, but abandoned, a little hurt by his abrupt departure. She dressed quickly, promising herself a long, lazy soak in the bath later, once the tank was full and the cows were milked, and ran downstairs just as he came back in.

'Everything seems all right. I've turned the lights off in the yard.'

'Thanks.'

'Tea?'

'I've put the kettle on.'

How ridiculous.

They'd been closer than she'd ever felt with anyone in her life, not just physically but emotionally, and now they were talking like polite acquaintances.

Hardly even that.

'Sam—'

'Jemima—'

They laughed awkwardly. 'You first,' he said.

She found a smile from somewhere. 'Thanks for last night,' she said gruffly. 'All of it—fishing me out of the river, warming me up—and afterwards. Staying with me. Holding me.' She hesitated, wondering if it was true. 'Loving me.'

He held out his arms and she went into them, fastening herself to him as if she would die without him. Odd. She felt as if she might, as if she would when he left. He was going now, she knew it, could feel it in the desperate hug he gave her.

'I have to go. I need to get back to London.'

She nodded and let him go, and he gathered his things together while she poured him a cup of tea, and then she watched him drink it too fast, scalding himself in his haste to get away.

'Leave it if it's too hot,' she said, and he put it down and went out, throwing his things into the back of the car.

She tugged on her boots and followed him out. At first she thought he was going to get into the driver's seat without saying goodbye, but in the end he reached for her and hugged her hard.

'I hate goodbyes,' he mumbled into her hair. 'Look after yourself, and stay away from the river. I'll be in touch.'

And then he was in the car, reversing smoothly out into the lane and pulling away, the car burbling gently, leaving a wisp of steam from its exhaust lingering in the air.

She did all the things she had to do—she checked the water pipes were all OK, did the milking, fed the dogs and took them for a run, went inside to have a bath, then got into her car and tried to start it so she could go and get some food from the village shop.

Nothing. Not so much as a glimmer of life. The engine turned over, but without the slightest urge to fire.

It was the last straw. She put her head down on the steering wheel and bawled her eyes out.

CHAPTER SEVEN

'JEMIMA?'

She lifted her head and looked round, to find Owen's familiar ruddy face where the door ought to be. 'You all right?' he asked, squatting down and regarding her thoughtfully.

'I'm fine,' she said, sniffing and dashing the tears off her cheeks with her sleeve. 'The damn car won't start, and I need to get to the shop to buy something to eat, and I'm running out of dog food, and the power's back on.'

'He's gone, hasn't he?' Owen said, and his big, rough hand cupped her knee and squeezed comfortingly while she fought back the stupid, stupid tears.

'I'm all right,' she said firmly, sniffing hard.

'Of course you are. Want a lift to the shops? I've got to go to the village for my mother—can't do damn all else with this blasted cast on, so I might as well run errands.'

She could sense the frustration in his voice, and thought they'd be good company for each other. Well matched, at the moment—both as miserable as sin.

'Thanks, Owen,' she mumbled, and he stood up to let her out of the car, then waited while she put the dogs inside and found her purse. His dog was in the back of the pick-up, waiting patiently, and wagged a greeting. She scratched its neck and climbed into the cab, then tried not to laugh at Owen's struggle with his cast and the gear lever.

'How is your arm?' she asked, when he swore softly and used the other hand to change gear.

'It'll do. Throbs a bit at night, but I suppose I got away lightly. Didn't do the tractor a lot of good, though, and I've had a lot of stick from the others. Can't understand it—it's not as if I haven't driven the darned thing in there enough times.'

'We all make mistakes,' Jemima assured him, and wondered if Sam would turn out to be one of hers.

They turned into the village street and pulled up outside the shop, and Owen's dog proceeded to hurl insults at a poodle that trotted past on a pretty little red lead. 'Oscar, shut up,' Owen growled, and the dog fell silent.

The village shop was heaving, of course, and Mary was there.

She smiled at Owen and drew Jemima on one side. 'Are you all right?' she asked softly.

'I'll live. I miss him already. It's ridiculous.'

Mary smiled mysteriously. 'He'll be back. Give him time to sort himself out—he's very busy at the minute, but once this project's all done and dusted, I think you'll find you're seeing a lot more of him.'

'Will I?' Jemima said quietly. 'His place is in London, Mary, not down here. He wanted me to go and see it, but how can I?'

Mary looked at Owen. 'I'm sure Owen would milk the cows for you over a weekend, and we'd have the dogs. Why don't you go up? I'm sure you'd find it fascinating.'

She shook her head. 'I can't.'

Mary shrugged. 'It's a shame—still, once it's finished I expect it will be in one of those magazines, anyway, and he's sent us all sorts of videos of it as it was and with the work in progress.'

'Has he?'

She couldn't help the brightening of her voice, and Mary smiled and patted her hand. 'I'll let you see them—come round and pick them up some time.'

'I will—Mary, I'd better go; Owen's waiting for me. My car wouldn't start.'

'You ought to do something about that,' she told Jemima. 'It'll let you down one day.'

'It just has,' she said drily, and Mary laughed.

'So get it fixed.'

'I can't afford to. No money.'

'Perhaps you should sell a few of the cows.'

'No. I'm not selling Uncle Tom's herd.'

'I keep offering to buy,' Owen said with a smile, overhearing their conversation. 'Fool woman won't part with them.'

'The fool woman likes them.'

Owen snorted, and Jemima winked at Mary. 'See you soon. Thanks for lending me Sam.'

'My pleasure. Don't forget to come and see us.'

'I will. I'll walk over.'

Owen took her home, and because it would be churlish to do anything else she offered him a cup of tea, and then instantly regretted it because he washed up Sam's mug and used it, and for some stupid, perverse reason she didn't want Owen touching it, even if it was only just a mug and even if he had been good to her—

'You love him, don't you?'

She lifted her head, startled, and met Owen's understanding eyes. 'Is it so obvious?' she said miserably.

Owen's mouth moved in a twisted little smile. 'Maybe only to me. Miss him already, don't you?'

'It's stupid. I've always known he lives in London—I knew he had to go back. It's just—I fell in the river last night and he pulled me out. If he hadn't, I would have drowned. I was too cold to help myself, and the current was so strong—'

She broke off, wrapping her arms round her waist, and then she felt herself folded against a hard masculine chest, the rigid bar of his plaster cast against her shoulders, his other hand patting her awkwardly.

'You might have died,' he said gruffly. 'Thank God he was here.' He sounded shocked, and almost guilty. Not another one. She had enough to deal with with Sam's guilt. She moved out of his awkward embrace.

'Owen, we're having an affair,' she told him bluntly, wanting him to know, but Owen just smiled ruefully and nodded.

'I know.'

'How do you know?' she asked indignantly.

He touched her top lip with a blunt finger. 'Whisker burn. Obvious to anyone with a brain what you two've been up to.' He shrugged. 'That's all right, it's your business. Just remember, if you need a shoulder, I'm here.'

'Owen, I'm never going to see you other than as a friend—'

'I know. Don't worry, it's all right. I'm only after your herd, anyway,' he said with a grin, and she knew then for sure that it wasn't true and that he did care about her.

'You're a sweetheart, Owen, do you know that?'

He flushed dark red and picked up his coat. 'Must be off—just remembered I have to go to the vet and pick up some antibiotics. I'll see you round—shout if you need anything, and stay away from that damn river.'

'Yes, Owen. Thank you.'

She watched him go, and then went upstairs and lay

down and buried her face in the pillow, breathing in the faint, lingering scent of Sam and remembering the feel of his arms around her and the leashed power of his body, holding back to give her time.

'I love you,' she whispered. 'Hurry back.'

Owen rang on Thursday to ask Jemima if she'd go to the pub with him that evening after she'd finished milking.

'Owen, I thought I told you—'

'You did. It's all right. Actually, I want you to help me,' he said, sounding embarrassed and diffident.

'Help you do what?' she asked suspiciously.

'There's a young lady in the pub—she works behind the bar. Jenny, her name is. I just wondered...'

'If I'd come with you and help you make her jealous? Oh, Owen, why don't you just tell her you like her?'

'Tried that a year ago.'

'A year—oh, Owen!'

He laughed sheepishly. 'So will you come?'

'Oh, all right, but just a quick drink. Pick me up at eight-thirty.'

Jenny did look jealous, Jemima noticed to her amazement. Every time Owen looked away, she looked across at him, and once she met Jemima's eye. Wow, Jemima thought, if looks could kill—

'I think you're in there, Owen, boy,' she said quietly, winking at him.

He went scarlet and buried his nose in the top of his pint. Jemima smiled and met the girl's glare with a level look of her own. It wouldn't hurt to give Owen a little ammunition. She put a hand on his arm. 'Shall we go?' she purred, and he looked startled for a second, then grinned.

'Right. Sure.'

They left, Jenny's eyes boring holes in them on the way out, and once in the car park Owen took his hand off her back and walked her to the car at a respectable distance.

'So, you reckon I stand a chance, do you?' he said with a grin as he started the engine.

'Probably. She didn't like seeing you with me.'

'Good.' He put the car in gear awkwardly with his good hand and pulled out onto the wet road. 'Heard any more from Sam?'

Her face fell, her enjoyment gone. 'No. I think he's rather busy. Some project that's coming to an end in a few weeks. I doubt if I'll see him for ages.'

She was wrong. He came down on Saturday, strolling over the hill with Dick and Mary's dogs in tow, but by then Jemima was having serious doubts about their relationship. She'd borrowed the videos from Mary and seen a little of what Sam was doing, and she was awe-struck. She'd watched them over and over again, as much as anything because he'd done a commentary over the top and she loved listening to his voice, but it was obvious that he loved his work and took huge pride in it, as well he might.

He was seriously talented, and she felt very provincial and boring by comparison. She wondered what on earth he could possibly see in her, and so she was a little reserved as she let him in.

Sam, though, had no such inhibitions. After greeting the dogs and shutting them all out together for a game in the garden, he pulled her gently into his arms and kissed her.

'I've missed you,' he murmured into her hair, and she felt her resolve disintegrate.

'I've missed you, too,' she confessed. 'How's the job going?'

'Oh, OK. On target, thank God.' He rested his chin on her head and sighed. 'I shall be glad in a way when it's all over.'

'It looks very exciting.'

He backed away and looked down at her. 'Grannie said she'd lent you the videos. I can't imagine why you're interested.'

Because it's you, she wanted to say, but stopped herself. 'I like old buildings,' she said instead, a little defensively. 'They fascinate me.'

He threw up his hands and laughed his surrender. 'OK, you don't have to justify yourself to me! I like old buildings too. That's why I tendered for the job.'

He looked out of the window at the dogs bouncing round the soggy garden. There was hardly a trace of snow left, just the odd grubby wedge of it tucked under a hedge where the sun couldn't get to it.

'Fancy walking the dogs?' he suggested.

She jumped at it. Apart from anything else, if they were out with the dogs they weren't shut up alone together, and she just felt they needed a little distance. 'Do I need to change?' she asked him, but he laughed and shook his head.

'To walk that lot? I doubt it. Where are we going?'

'Along the river? It's very lovely and we can cut back over the hill about a mile down and come back round the other side, past your grandparents.'

'OK.' He called the dogs while she put her coat on and found some thick socks for her wellies, then they set off over the river and along the far bank. Sam looked relaxed, she thought, his hands in his pockets, the sun on his face, the dogs bouncing all around him—he didn't look like a city slicker today, and she wondered if she'd misjudged him.

They had a wonderful walk. He talked about the building project, and how much time was left, and what might go wrong, and she realised that, talented though he was, he was under enormous pressure to come in on time and under budget.

And she got stressed if she was half an hour late to milk her cows!

She realised how far she'd distanced herself from the fast lane in the past year, and wondered if she loved Sam enough to risk going back to it for him.

'It's so gorgeous here,' he said suddenly, and she knew it would be a very hard choice to make. Maybe even impossible. She just hoped she never had to make it, but that would mean losing Sam, and it gave her a terrible, hollow ache inside just to think about it.

'I love it,' she told him. 'I hated London—all the rich, spoilt people squabbling over their children and bickering about access and who would have the children for Christmas as if they were just commodities. It sickened me, Sam.'

He nodded. 'I know what you mean. I'm finding it a bit of a two-edged sword living on the site now, since the award nomination. All the people that collect designer labels and flash their wealth around are suddenly at the front of my queue, wanting extensions to their pretentious houses and new and more elaborate roof gardens and bijou little coach house conversions—none of them are truly interested in design; they just want me dangling from their belts like another scalp, and it's really not my thing.'

'So tell them that.'

He laughed a little bitterly. 'I would, but work isn't

that guaranteed or plentiful. The competition is cut-throat, and I can't be sure I'll get every job I tender for by a long shot. I'm not rich enough to tell them all to sling their hooks.'

'So what would you rather be doing?' she asked curiously.

'Oh, interesting domestic stuff—one-offs on crazy sites, conversions of listed buildings to dwellings—that sort of thing. I really enjoyed designing the flats, creating an unusual living space out of a huge barn of a place. It was fun finding something unusual to do.'

'So not necessarily commercial, then?'

'Oh, no.' He shook his head thoughtfully. 'It was a challenge, but domestic architecture is what really interests me. Fitting the house to the person. There are fewer constraints, and they tend not to be so grittily financial. Commerce nearly always comes down to the bottom line.'

She laughed. 'And domestic architecture doesn't?'

'Not at the level I'm talking about. There are people who know just what they want and will pay for it, regardless. Not many, but hopefully enough.'

'The award should help you there, surely?'

'If I win it, which is by no means certain.' He laughed wryly. 'All those women who want me dangling from their belts will be gutted if I don't.'

'And you?' she asked, watching him carefully. 'Will you be gutted?'

His face sobered. 'I don't know. Probably. It's a pat on the back from your colleagues—that's always good to have. But whoever wins it will deserve it and the nomination itself is a tremendous honour.'

They walked on in silence for a while, the dogs sniffing about in the hedgerows and chasing each other across the fields, and then they turned and headed over the steep wooded hillside.

'I thought I was fit,' Sam gasped, sagging against a tree and laughing. He flopped over so his hands were on his knees, and drew several deep breaths before straightening up and grinning. 'You aren't even breathing hard!'

She grinned back. 'That's because I don't sit at a drawing board all day.'

'Nor do I!' he protested. 'I run around on the site, up ladders and round scaffolding—I never have time to sit about for long.'

'You need to do some more mucking out to keep you toned.'

'Hah! You don't catch me with that one,' he said with a laugh. 'Haven't you got your tractor fixed yet?'

Her face must have fallen, because his brows drew together in a frown and he leant back against the tree, regarding her thoughtfully. 'Is the money really that tight?' he asked with customary bluntness.

'What do you think? I had to pour all my milk down the drain for four days, and things were already tight. I really couldn't afford that power cut, never mind having to get the tractor fixed—and my car's on the blink, just as if things weren't bad enough.'

He looked down at his hands, studying them intently. 'Do you need a loan?'

'No!'

He looked up and met her eyes, and his own were filled with understanding. 'Interest free?' he suggested.

She thought of the mortgage she'd had to take out to pay off Uncle Tom's debts—the mortgage that was threatening to make her lose her home and her livelihood. 'I can't afford to repay it.'

'So have it as a gift.'

She shouldered away from the tree she was leaning against. 'What's the matter, Sam? Still feeling guilty because I fell in the river?'

He gave a sharp sigh and fell into step behind her. 'Don't be stupid! I just meant—well, I hate to see you struggling.'

She laughed bitterly. 'That's farming, Sam. Don't forget, I can always sell the herd and go back to soliciting.'

There was a startled cough of laughter from behind her, and she turned round with a slight smile. 'My brother's joke. That's what he used to tell people I did. When I got my first job he told everyone I'd started soliciting to support myself. My parents found out when some friends of theirs rang up scandalised.'

His mouth curved in a smile, but his eyes were still concerned. She laid a hand on his arm.

'Sam, I'm fine. Don't worry about me. I'll get by. Things are always grim at the end of the winter. In the summer, when I don't have to feed the stock, things will look up.'

He regarded her steadily, then nodded. 'OK—but if you do need anything, just to bail you out for a spell or whatever, just ask.'

She nodded, her throat tight. 'Thanks.' She turned back to the path and headed on up to the top of the hill. She was on the verge of tears, and it would have been so easy to turn round and go into his arms and let him take care of all her problems for her.

But Jemima wasn't a quitter, so she struggled on to the top of the hill, looked out over the folded green Dorset landscape and thanked her lucky stars that, whatever else beset her, she could still appreciate the beauty of her surroundings.

'Wow,' Sam breathed, awestruck. 'That is just spectacular.'

'Lovely, isn't it? Look, down there is your grandparents' place, and there's my farm—you can see the cattle.'

He was right beside her, so close that she could smell the subtle tang of his aftershave. His hand was on her shoulder and he peered along her arm, seeing where she pointed.

'Is that the village?'

'Yes—you can see the pub and the church just beyond it.'

'It seems familiar. Did we come up here as kids?'

'Oh, always. We used to play in the woods. Uncle Tom used to get frantic because we'd all be gone for hours.'

Sam laughed ruefully. 'I seem to remember getting a hiding from my grandfather for being back late and landing you in trouble.'

She chuckled. 'I wouldn't remember. I had so many hidings for being back late they all run into a blur—which reminds me, I have to get back to do the milking, so we ought to press on.' She headed off down the hill, whistling up the dogs, and cut across the pasture towards Dick and Mary's farmhouse.

It was quicker downhill, although harder on the legs, and they arrived with just time for a quick cup of tea before she needed to head back.

'Sam can run you and the dogs back in the Land Rover,' Dick suggested. 'That way you'll have time for two cups.'

So she stayed for two cups, and Sam ran her back in the battered old farm Land Rover that not even the dogs could ruin, and as they pulled into the yard he turned to her.

'Are you busy tonight after you finish milking?'

She thought of all the things she could be doing, and how much she wanted to be with Sam, and shook her head. 'No, not really.'

'Fancy dinner at the pub? Nothing flashy, just a bar snack if you don't feel like dressing up, or we could splash out and go into Dorchester if you'd rather.'

She thought of her wardrobe, and her hands that were not really fit to appear in public, and shook her head. 'The pub would be lovely,' she told him. 'Don't dress up; I haven't got anything except jeans and business suits.'

He laughed. 'I'll wear jeans. I'll see you—when? Eight?'

'That's fine,' she said, and wondered if she was being silly, allowing their relationship to develop when there was clearly no future in it. She got out of the Land Rover and he leant across, grinning.

'I don't suppose you want company while you milk?'

'What, are you missing it, Sam?' she teased, and he laughed.

'Oh, yeah—and especially Daisy's back end.'

She gave a little spurt of laughter. 'Poor Daisy.'

'Poor nothing. Can I stay?'

'Sure—if you want to. Uncle Tom's wellies are where you left them.'

He put them on, and the old coat he'd worn, while she poured water from the kettle into a bucket and fed the dogs. While she forked silage into the troughs and started up the milking machine, Sam prowled around, peering into the cooling tank and examining all the now functional machinery.

'Is it quicker now it's working properly?' he asked as she linked up the first cow to the suction cups.

'A bit. It still takes time—a more modern milking parlour would be far more efficient, but this does us.' She straightened. 'Did I ever really thank you for fixing the little Lister engine for me?'

He moved closer, a sexy, lazy smile playing around his lips. 'You could always thank me again,' he murmured, and drew her into his arms.

The first brush of his lips was like the kiss of rain in the desert, and like a desert flower she opened to his touch. He gave a low groan and deepened the kiss, his hands coming up to cup her head and steady it against the onslaught of his mouth, and her legs turned to jelly.

He shifted, propping her against the wall, only the wall wasn't a wall, it was Daisy, and she gave a disapproving moo and sidestepped.

Sam staggered, hauling Jemima up against his front, and she laughed and turned her head and returned the cow's level stare.

'Daisy, you're such a prude,' she lectured, and Sam chuckled and let her go.

'Later,' he promised, and fire smouldered in his eyes.

Jemima felt her heart kick against her ribs, and turned back to the cows, concentrating on her job. At least, she tried, but Sam was there, propping up the wall, watching her with those smoky, sexy eyes, and all she could think about was what would happen later.

'If you've got nothing better to do you could always muck out,' she advised him, straightening up from the third cow to find him still there watching her.

'Muck out?' he said in dismay, and, shutting his eyes, he let out a low, humourless laugh. 'How did I know there'd be a catch?'

'No catch. I can muck out, but I'll be very tired later.'

His eyes widened, and he shouldered himself away from the wall and grinned. 'Where's the barrow?'

'On the muck heap.'

He went, and moments later he was back again, whistling softly and forking up the soiled straw with what looked almost like enthusiasm.

'Just think how fit you'll be,' she teased, and he gave a grunt of laughter.

'Fit to drop. Just warn Daisy, if she squirts me this time she'll be casseroled!'

The pub was heaving. They found a space in the corner near the fire, and ordered jacket potatoes filled with tuna and mayonnaise. Jemima was starving, and she knew from past experience that the jacket potatoes were a good size.

Which was just as well, because apart from the odd bit of toast she hadn't eaten for two days. She really must get to the shops!

The landlord brought their meals to them, and looked down at Jemima with a grin. 'You're a popular young lady this week! First Owen, now this young man. I don't know, spoilt for choice!'

And he smacked their plates down and vanished into the crowd.

Sam looked at her oddly. 'Owen?' he said softly.

Absurdly, she felt guilty. 'He brought me in here on Thursday for a drink.' She thought of telling him about Jenny, but decided not to. It seemed a bit unfair to Owen.

Sam, however, had gone very quiet and was looking wary.

'Sam? He's a friend. It doesn't mean anything.'

'Doesn't it? He was pretty keen to get rid of me.'

She sighed and stabbed her fork into her potato, mashing it angrily. 'Look, it was nothing. OK? Now let's forget it.'

Sam couldn't forget it, though. He looked strained and unhappy all through their meal, and pushed his plate away half finished. Jemima cleaned hers up, looked at him and pointed at the plate with her fork. 'You finished with that?'

He slid it across the table to her and sat back, folding his arms. 'Be my guest,' he said drily, and watched her as she demolished the remains of his meal.

'I don't know where you put it,' he remarked as she swallowed the last bite. She met his eyes and found them cynical and a little hurt, and she put the fork down and leant towards him.

'Look, Owen asked me to come with him—'

'It's none of my business why you were here with Owen; you've made that perfectly clear.'

'—because he fancies the girl—oh, hello, Jenny.'

'Getting around, aren't you?' the girl said, gathering up their plates. 'Can I bring you any dessert?'

'Apple pie and cream, please. Sam?'

'Ditto. I'm sure you can eat mine.'

Jenny sniffed and ran her eyes over Sam, then winked at him and went off with their plates.

'She's the girl Owen fancies. He's been trying to screw up the courage to ask her out for a year. He wanted me to come with him to make her jealous, as everything else seems to have failed. That's why I was here, and it's the only reason.'

Sam looked down at his glass and swirled the slice of lemon round in the mineral water. 'I'm sorry. I should have given you the benefit of the doubt. I'm not normally jealous, there's just something about Owen—or maybe it's you. You seem to bring out a possessive streak in me I didn't know I had. I'm probably just tired.'

She smiled. 'That's OK. I should have explained.'

Jenny brought their apple pie then, and Sam attacked his like a man possessed.

'I'm starving now,' he confessed, and she realised that the thought of her with Owen had put him off his food.

'What a shame,' she teased. 'I was looking forward to eating yours.'

'Tough,' he mumbled, and scooped up the last mouthful.

She had hardly swallowed when he stood up and went to the bar to pay the bill, then led her out.

'Where's the fire?' she asked, and he laughed softly under his breath.

'Need you ask?'

He helped her into the car with a natural courtesy she found rather touching, and then whisked her home along the lanes, pulling up in the yard outside her cottage in what was beginning to feel like his spot.

Then he ushered her down the path, grumbled about the lack of outside lights and stood so close behind her that she could hardly concentrate well enough to get the key in the lock.

The dogs greeted them with enthusiasm, mugging Sam again as if they hadn't seen him for ages instead of two hours ago, and Jemima put them out, put the kettle on and turned to him.

'Tea or coffee?'

His eyes burned with need. 'Neither. I just want to hold you. It feels like for ever since I held you last.'

'Oh, Sam...'

She pulled the kettle off the hob and went into his

arms. 'I've missed you,' she mumbled against his coat. 'It seems crazy after just one weekend, but—I don't know.'

'I agree. I don't know why it is either, but it is.' He tipped her head up and stared down into her eyes, searching them. She wondered if he would see the aching vulnerability, the weakness she felt for him, the terrible need that would make her weep when he left again—

'Come to bed.'

His voice was gruff, a little scratchy, and it did away with any good intentions she might have had about slowing things down and taking their time to get to know each other.

She just wanted him, needed him—loved him.

She let the dogs in, gave them a biscuit and led Sam upstairs. The bedroom door had hardly clicked shut before he reached for her, desire blazing in his eyes, making his hands tremble and his breathing ragged.

All the things, in fact, that were happening to her.

'Sam—'

'Jemima—'

Their soft groans were lost in the white heat of that first kiss, their clothes thrust aside impatiently. And then the tempo slowed, as if holding was the first and most important thing on his mind, and everything else would just follow naturally.

'You feel so good,' he groaned roughly, his hands caressing her, touching her tenderly, driving her wild with need.

She thought she'd scream when he paused for a moment to protect her, but then he was with her again, soaring on that crazy spiral that left them breathless and shaken in each other's arms.

'Sam?' she whispered.

'I know,' he said, and he sounded choked. 'I know, sweetheart.'

And his arms closed around her, cradling her protectively against his pounding heart...

CHAPTER EIGHT

'SOMETHING occurs to me.'

Sam's voice was a low rumble under her ear. Jemima snuggled closer, enjoying the feel of his warm, hard body against hers. 'Mmm?'

'The other night, when you fell in the river—we weren't thinking too clearly. I don't suppose there's any possibility that you're pregnant?'

Pregnant? Good grief, she hadn't thought at all, never mind clearly! 'Um,' she said slowly, trying to think. 'I don't know—I don't think so. It was the last thing on my mind at the time, I must admit.'

His arm tightened protectively. 'Mine too—I was just too busy getting used to the idea that you were warm and still breathing to worry about anything else.' He hesitated. 'You're not—um—on the pill or anything?'

She shook her head. 'No—there wasn't any need.'

'So, do you think there's a chance?' he asked softly, and if she hadn't known better she'd have thought he sounded almost hopeful.

He waited, hardly seeming to breathe, until she thought he must be able to feel her mind whirling. 'I don't know,' she confessed. It didn't surprise her. She was too busy to worry about nature, and with no reason to pay attention to her cycle, she had only a vague idea.

'You will tell me?'

She thought of her body cradling Sam's child, and a dull, almost biological ache seemed to fill her. 'I doubt if I am,' she said, finally remembering that it had been early in her cycle. Tonight, though, was probably right on target, so it was a good job he'd thought of it, because once again her mind had been in neutral.

He turned towards her, lying so that they were face to face, and stared into her eyes. 'I have to go soon,' he murmured. 'I told my grandparents not to expect me back—I said I'd leave after we'd had dinner. I've got so much to do for this opening it's just ridiculous.'

He looked preoccupied already, and Jemima could feel him slipping away from her.

'How about that coffee we were going to have before you go?' she suggested, trying to stall the inevitable.

'I've got a better idea.' His lips brushed hers, warm and soft and tender, and she shut her mind to the fact that he was leaving and just enjoyed the last few moments she would have with him before he went back to his clamouring world.

He rang her on Sunday morning, just as she finished the milking, to tell her he was back safely. He was on a mobile phone, and she could hear clanging and banging in the background.

'Look, sorry, I'm going to have to go. I'm on site, and someone needs me. I'll speak to you soon. Take care.'

'And you.' She cradled the phone, her eyes misting over. It was crazy, but she missed him.

She watched the videos again, just to torture herself, and then took the dogs for a walk up the hill. She sat on a log, looking out over the village and the fields she loved, and missed him.

When she came down it was time to milk again, and after she'd finished, and done the hens and checked the calves, she went inside and threw together a sandwich and ate it alone, with just the dogs for company. Then, because she hadn't had a great deal of sleep what with one thing and another, she went to bed—and missed him.

'You are going to have to get a grip,' she told herself sternly. She rolled over, punched the pillow into shape and rested her face on it—and there was the lingering trace of his aftershave to torture her. She buried her nose in the pillow and breathed deeply, and let the memories wash over her.

Sam might have gone back to London, but his image was still there with her, as clear as day. If she closed her eyes she could hear his laughter, the soft rumble of his voice, the ragged catch of his breath when she touched him—

She sat up and turned on the light, and reached for a book. She'd been halfway through it when Sam arrived nine days ago—heavens, was it really only nine days?—and she hadn't had a chance to get back to it. Perhaps it would take her mind off him...

'Jemima?'

She felt a silly grin light up her face, and curled up in a chair by the phone, hugging the receiver lovingly. 'Hi, Sam,' she said, giddy with relief that he'd phoned at last.

'Are you OK?'

'I'll manage. How's the building coming on? Are they on target?'

He sighed shortly. 'Oh, more or less. We've had the odd hiccup.' There was a pause, then he said, 'I miss you.'

'I miss you, too. You seem a very long way away.'

He laughed, a brittle, humourless laugh. 'I might as

well be in Siberia. Look—' He let his breath out in a rush. 'I don't suppose there's any chance you could come up for the opening, is there? It's next week—Friday night.'

'Me?' she squeaked.

'Don't sound so surprised. Why not you? I thought you might be interested to see it, and—well, to be honest, I need a cheerleader. It's going to be hell, and frankly I'm scared to death.'

'And you want someone to comfort you?'

He chuckled. 'Share it with me, perhaps. Just be there for me.'

'What about your parents?'

'They're coming, but it's not the same. I want your support, but I also want to celebrate. It would just be nice to have *you* here.'

She chewed her lip thoughtfully. 'Sam, I'll have to see if Owen can do the cows. His arm's still in plaster, and he can't do a lot, but he might be able to manage just them if it was only a night. I suppose I could come back down on the Saturday morning—'

'I'll drive you back—I'd come down and pick you up but I'm going to be a bit on the busy side on Friday afternoon.'

'I'll get the train. That's not a problem. Let me talk to Owen and your grandparents. If I can farm out the animals, I'll do it. I'd love to come.'

'Wonderful. I can't wait. Look, I've got to fly; I've got to go and check a few things before tomorrow and do some work on another project. I'll be in touch. Take care.'

'And you. Bye.' She cradled the phone gently and told herself it was only ten days. Then it dawned on her what she'd let herself in for, and with a little yelp she ran upstairs and rummaged through her wardrobe.

Nothing. Well, nothing suitable for such a grand event.

She sat down on the edge of the bed and thought of the money she'd got stashed away to fix the tractor. There was a nearly-new designer clothes shop in Dorchester. If she bought something there and wore it once, she could take it back and sell it again and only lose the commission—

Mmm. Good idea. She'd go tomorrow.

No. She'd contact Owen and Mary, and if she managed to arrange babysitters for the dogs and the cows, then and only then would she go and blow her tractor repair money on a dress.

And while she was at it she'd take in some of her power suits that she had no need for any more...

Jemima leant her arms on the top of the gate, propped her foot on the bottom rung and smiled at Owen. 'So, how's it going with Jenny?'

He laughed and came over to her, abandoning his one-handed silage forking. 'She tells me you were in there with Sam—I seem to feel that really annoyed her.'

Jemima chuckled. 'I think so. She wiggled at Sam, just to irritate me.'

'And did it?'

'No.' She looked up at him, propped on the gate beside her. 'Owen, I wanted to ask you a favour.'

His face brightened. 'Want me to buy the cows?'

'In your dreams,' she said with a laugh. 'No. I want you to milk them. Sam's been involved in the conversion of some old buildings in London, and it's the official opening next Friday night. I wondered if you'd do the milking Friday night and Saturday morning. I'll be back by lunchtime.'

Owen pulled at his jaw and stared at the sky. 'Well, now, let me see. I suppose—I might be able to,' he said, turning back to her with a twinkle. 'Seeing as it's you, and as this fellow seems to have got right under your skin.'

She hugged him over the gate. 'I'll do the hens before I go and after I get back, and I'll make sure the cows are in ready. There really won't be a lot to do.'

'I used to help Tom out now and then—don't suppose you do it much different?'

'No. I'm sure you can cope, Owen.'

'Oh, I expect I might.' He leant on the gate and studied her thoughtfully. 'What're you going to do if he asks you to marry him?'

'Marry him?' She blinked, totally astonished. 'Well—I don't know. I haven't thought about it. It's a little early for that; I hardly know him.'

'Hmm,' Owen said, and she went to Dorchester on the bus, armed with her tractor repair money, and pondered on the idea that Sam might propose.

Crazy. Of course he wouldn't. It was just a quick affair, probably a bit of time out from the hectic countdown to the opening.

She felt curiously disappointed.

The dress shop was through a walkway under the upper floor of an old terrace, in the mews area at the back. It was only a single floor, but there were lots of wonderful things. Some of them must have been mind-bogglingly expensive to start with, Jemima thought, flicking through the rail.

She knew just what she wanted—something black and

simple and totally demure—and she finally found it hidden amongst a clutch of cocktail dresses. Sleeveless, it had a simple, fairly high round neck at the front, a cross-over back with a little keyhole between the shoulder blades and it ended just above the knee.

It was utterly simple, it fitted her like a charm and she loved it to pieces.

It also took nearly all of her tractor repair money, leaving just enough to splash out on some full-length sheer black gloves that covered her mangled hands all the way up to the armpit. She had some simple black court shoes that would do the job, and with a pair of slinky nearly black sheer tights, she'd be away.

Excellent.

She had a few minutes before the bus, so she pottered up and down looking in the estate agents. Spring was making itself felt, she noticed. There were adverts asking for farmhouses and cottages, couples who were desperate and had sold their own and had cash waiting, and she saw a farm similar to hers for much more than hers had been valued at for probate purposes.

She thought how lucky she'd been, because if it had been valued at any more she wouldn't have been able to keep it because she couldn't have afforded the inheritance tax.

The bus came and took her back, and she hung her new dress up in the wardrobe with the gloves, changed into her scruffy work clothes and went to do the milking.

A letter arrived for her the following Tuesday, containing a train ticket for Friday afternoon, telling her a taxi, already paid for, would pick her up at two-thirty, and Sam would meet her at the station in London.

It was from his secretary, and she felt a pang of regret

that it wasn't from him personally until he rang up late that night. She was woken by the phone and stumbled down the stairs, grabbing the receiver.

'Hello?' she mumbled breathlessly.

'Hi. Are you all right?' he asked, sounding concerned.

'Fine. Just sleepy. I'd gone to bed.'

He swore softly. 'I'm sorry, I forgot how early you turn in. Did you get the ticket from Val?'

'Yes—thanks. Owen and your grandparents are all programmed—Sam, how dressy is this?' she asked, suddenly panicking about her second-hand dress.

'Dressy? Well, fairly, I suppose. A formal cocktail dress will be ideal, I would have thought, but really anything goes, just so long as it's fairly smart. Is that a problem?'

She thought of her languishing tractor. 'No, no problem,' she lied. Anyway, the money was spent, the dress sounded right and she did look good in it. It would be nice to see Sam's face—

'How's it going?' she asked.

'Oh—you know. I'm shattered. I'm really looking forward to it all being over so I can get some sleep, but there's another project butting up behind it—oh, hell, I don't know. Look, I have to go; I've got tons to do. I'm sorry I woke you, but I wanted to check you'd got the ticket. Take care. I'll see you on Friday.'

She thought Friday would never come. She got up at stupid o'clock, milked the cows early and turned them out, mucked out the barn, fed the calves and hens, collected the eggs, delivered the dogs to Mary and Dick, brought the cows back in, leapt into the bath, scrubbed herself rapidly, hurled on one of her remaining business suits for the journey and put the dress, gloves and shoes into the top of her case.

Then she went downstairs, looked longingly at the loaf of bread on the side and glanced at her watch.

No time. The taxi pulled up in the yard and honked, and she was off. The train was on time, and she emerged from the station just as Sam got out of a taxi and waved to her.

'Jemima!'

She broke into a run, absurdly pleased to see him, and he hugged her and whirled her round, setting her down on her feet and standing back to look at her. 'Good grief—it's the first time I've seen you without a thin film of farmyard—you clean up well!'

She laughed and hit him, just gently, and he hugged her again and picked up her bag, hurrying her to the taxi. 'The traffic's hell, and I couldn't face trying to get the car out. Come on, I've still got masses to do.'

The taxi cut and swerved through the stop-go rush hour traffic, finally turning into a gravelled courtyard in the centre of some tall brick buildings. People were scurrying in all directions, setting out tubs of plants, hanging banners, checking lights—it was a hive of activity, and Sam ushered her through it all into a glass enclosure between two of the buildings.

It was spectacular, lush with plants, filled with light and air and space, and already she was in love with it. An oval glass lift carried them up to the top, and they stepped out onto a walkway that led into one of the buildings.

'This is home,' Sam said, and, slipping a key into the lock, he pushed the door aside and ushered her in.

Her jaw dropped. The ceiling was way above them, soaring up into the roof beams, and the overall impression was of light. White walls, blond wood, black iron and old roof timbers dominated, and here and there were old bits of machinery still in place—a chute, a hopper, a rake on the wall—remnants of the original trade that had been plied here.

The far end was divided into two floors. Stairs rose ahead of them, plate glass sheets taking the place of balusters under the maple banister rail, so that she could see the upper floor, and at the end of it a door out onto a balcony.

The end they had come in at was a working area, the studio where she imagined he spent long hours over the drawing board and on the phone hustling builders. There was work in progress on the drawing board, a neat stack of drawings on a plan chest, photos pinned to a wall board. It looked busy and organised and a little daunting.

The upper floor seemed to be a living area, with low sofas upholstered in pale split hide artfully arranged around a low central table. She imagined the havoc Jess would cause on the butter-coloured suede after a walk, and bit her lip.

It was immaculate, not a thing out of place, the walls festooned with dynamic pictures—all originals, no doubt—everything beautifully understated and tasteful.

She thought of her kitchen, where she and Sam had spent so many hours, and wondered how he could tolerate it when he was used to this.

'Well?'

'It's stunning—gorgeous,' she said, rather dazed, and he hugged her.

'Look, I have to fly. I'll be back in a bit. The kitchen's down here. Help yourself to anything you want—make some tea. I'll be back in a jiff.'

He went, leaving her alone, and she wandered through to the kitchen, still feeling a little dazed. It was beautiful, pale maple and stainless steel and gleaming glass, and she thought again of her kitchen, with the Rayburn that must be fifty years old, and her confidence started to wither.

She put the kettle on—a beautifully shaped, almost sculptured object in stainless steel that could have graced a mantelpiece—and while it boiled she wandered through the rest of the flat.

His bedroom was as she might have expected—neat, tidy, very simple, with a balcony overlooking the river and its own bathroom. Again, the suite looked as if it had been chosen as much for form as function. The taps were graceful arches, the china smooth curves, the bath huge.

She went up to the sitting area and perched on the edge of one of the sofas, smoothing it with her fingertips. Butter-soft as well as butter-coloured.

The kettle clicked, and she went down and made a cup of tea, taking it back up and standing by the balcony doors, looking out over the river. It was dusk now, not so dark yet that she couldn't see the ugliness of a big city, but once night fell, with the lights twinkling on the water, it would be lovely.

She finished her tea, washed up the mug and put it away, and then looked around for a hanger for her dress.

She found one in a wardrobe in his room—a wardrobe that contained suits, smart casual clothes, expensive jackets—all the trappings of a big-time successful man of the world.

She thought of Uncle Tom's old waxed jacket, and cringed. She must have been mad to think he could see anything in her but a minor and convenient diversion, their lovemaking recompense for the long hours she'd made him work in her barn.

Tears stung her eyes, and she was about to stuff the

dress back into the suitcase and run away when he came back and found her.

'OK?' he asked, and pulled her into his arms without waiting for an answer. 'God, you feel so good. I've missed you so much. Any tea in the pot?'

She laughed shakily. 'I made it in a mug. Do you want some?'

'Love some. I haven't had time to stop all day. So, what do you think of the flat?'

'Beautiful,' she said honestly, and knew she couldn't run out on him now, not just before the opening. Anyway, she was here now. She might as well see what he'd done to the rest...

'Look, I'm going to have to go back down before this thing starts. Why don't you just get yourself all done up in your own time and come down for seven-thirty? I'll meet you at the entrance.'

She felt a flutter of panic, and suppressed it. She was a big girl now, and she'd done far worse things, like standing up in court and representing her devious and conniving clients—

'Sure,' she said with a smile, and he dropped a kiss on her lips and jack-knifed out of the settee.

'I'll go and have a shower and get ready, then, and you can have the bathroom and bedroom to yourself.'

He disappeared, emerging about half an hour later looking immaculate in a dinner suit and a blindingly white shirt with pin-tucks down the front. The only sour note was the wrinkled rag that dangled round his neck.

'You any good with bow ties?' he growled up the stairs.

She hid a smile and put down the magazine she'd been flicking through. 'I might be. Got an iron?'

He muttered something dark and disappeared again. She followed him, finding him in the kitchen pulling out a retracting iron board from one of the cupboards. The iron was on and plugged in, and she set it to the right temperature for silk and waited a moment, smoothing out the creases.

He fretted while the iron heated up. He looked at his watch, glared at the iron, drummed his fingers on the black granite worktop and brought a smile to her lips.

'Don't panic.'

'I am panicking. I need to be down there again in five minutes and this thing's going to take ages to tie—'

'Nonsense. Clean handkerchief?'

'Are you asking if I've got one or do you want to blow your nose?'

She sighed and held out her hand, and he smacked a clean, folded white square into it. She damped it and laid it on the bow tie, then ran the iron lightly over it, finishing the handkerchief off before handing it back folded as before.

'Here you go, precious.'

His mouth tightened, but she wouldn't let him fluster her. She'd been the only one in the family who could tie her father's bow tie, and as he'd had a lot of dress functions to attend in her adolescence, she'd had scads of practice.

'Stand still,' she commanded softly, and with a few deft flicks and a tug she had it done.

'Just like that?' he growled sceptically, and she smiled.

'Just like that. Go on, then, off you go.'

'You know where to go? Down in the lift, turn left into the courtyard and follow the hullaballoo. I'll meet you in the foyer at seven-thirty.'

He cupped her cheeks in his hands, dropped a quick, hard kiss on her lips and let her go with obvious reluctance. 'Here goes,' he murmured, and she picked a little bit of lint off his shoulder and kissed him again.

'Good luck.'

'Thanks.' He smiled, but the strain showed around his eyes and she knew he was dreading it. He still hadn't had any news about the design award, and he'd been expecting it this week. It was just another thing adding to the strain, she realised, and she wondered if it was just her that found his lifestyle anathema.

She ran the bath and wallowed in the huge and glorious tub, revelling in the spa system that massaged her with powerful bubbles and jets of water and eased out all the kinks and creases. Then, conscious of the time, she washed her hair, towelled it roughly dry, put on her make-up and underwear, all bar the stockings that her hands would shred, then slid into the dress, taking care not to put make-up on the neckline as she squiggled into it.

It was a two-person job, really, but she managed it, zipped it up and then frowned in the mirror. Her hair was dry, its usual wildly curly self but gleaming with health since she had a sensible diet and plenty of fresh air.

It was also well tangled. She combed it through carefully, wincing as it tugged, scrunched it with some mousse and then turned her attention to her hands.

Hmm. A dead giveaway to her lifestyle! Still, at least her war-wounds were honestly come by. She put lavish amounts of handcream on, gave it a few moments to sink in, then buried the evidence inside the gloves. She giggled as she drew them up. The only other person she knew who wore gloves this long was the vet!

Oh, dear. Were her animals all right? Perhaps she ought to ring Owen—

'You're being daft. What can you do about it anyway?' she told herself, and after putting on her stockings with her gloved hands she stood back to study the finished job.

Wow. Even she could see that she looked good. She wondered what Sam would say, and found she couldn't wait to find out. She was ready—why not go down?

She made sure she had everything, and she was just on the way out when the phone rang. She paused a moment, then the answer-phone picked it up. She stayed to listen to the message in case it was important, and then flew out of the flat, slamming the door behind her and diving into the lift. It glided down altogether too slowly, and as soon as it stopped she shot out of it and almost ran across the courtyard in her haste.

A liveried doorman stopped her in the foyer. 'Good evening, madam. Could I see your ticket, please?'

She stared at him blankly. 'Ticket? I don't have a ticket. I'm with Sam Bradley.'

The man smiled. 'Nice try, madam. I'm afraid Mr Bradley's guests all have tickets.'

'Well, I don't—'

'Apparently not.'

She rolled her eyes in frustration and clung to her temper with difficulty. 'Please, you don't understand. I've just come down from his flat—he said he'd meet me here at seven-thirty.'

'It's only seven-ten, madam. If what you say is correct, I suggest you wait for him here.'

'Can't you find him for me?'

The doorman shook his head. 'I'm sorry, madam, he's busy at the moment. I can't disturb him—'

'But I need to speak to him! I've got something to tell him!' she said urgently. She scanned the crowd forming behind the man through the big doors, and there amongst them she caught sight of him.

'Sam!' she called, and he turned his head and waved. Detaching himself from the crowd he made his way across to her and hugged her, then stood back and looked at her.

'Wow, you look stunning! Come on, there are lots of people you've got to meet.' And without giving her a chance to say a word he towed her across the floor and started introducing her to the rest of the design team, the building contractor who'd done the work, and a host of others whose names she instantly forgot.

She tried to interrupt him, but there was no chance, and every time there was the slightest lull someone else jumped in.

She tugged his sleeve. 'Sam, I have to talk to you—'

'Later—the civic dignitaries have arrived. Stand by for the official hoo-hah.' He turned to greet them, and she sighed with frustration and wondered how on earth she could get his attention.

Inspiration struck. 'Have you got a pen?' she asked one of the design team, and he handed her a ball-point. Without further ado she rolled down her left glove, wrote on her forearm and shoved it under Sam's nose.

He glanced down, frowning slightly, did a distinct double take and turned to her, ignoring the rather pompous official he'd been talking to.

'What do you mean?' he asked, sounding slightly stunned.

'Sam, I was just coming out of your flat when the phone rang—you've done it! You've got the award!'

'What?'

The colour drained from his face, and shock held him rigid. 'What?' he said again, and she repeated what she'd heard.

'They'd just come out of the meeting and they wanted you to know before tonight, because they knew it was the official opening. They said they'd try your mobile—someone called Carol something—Carter?'

'Cartwright,' he said slowly, and deep in his eyes the joy started to shine. 'We've done it. My God, we've done it! We've won!'

'Well done,' she said softly, and, going up on tiptoe, she laid a kiss on his lips.

He laughed and hugged her, whirling her round, and when he put her down and she looked up from his shining eyes, the civic dignitaries were standing looking bemused just a few feet from them.

'Sorry, gentlemen. I've just been told we've won the design award—a message was left on my answerphone.'

There was a hubbub of back-slapping and congratulations, and into it all walked his parents—at least, she assumed they were his parents. The man was older, but the spitting image of Sam, and the woman had his eyes and the same smile.

'Well done, Sam,' his father said, pumping his hand, but his mother pulled a handkerchief out of her bag and told him to stand still.

'You've got lipstick on,' she said, dabbing at it, and then she hugged him, unable to hide her pride any longer, and Jemima sniffed and smiled and tried to remember if her mascara was waterproof...!

CHAPTER NINE

IT WAS the last conversation she had with him for ages. Everybody wanted to talk to him, and news of the award spread like wildfire through the crowd. Jemima stood beside him, spoke when she was spoken to and looked around at the wonderful theatre building and the things Sam had done to it.

It was fascinating, full of warmth and character, and she could imagine how popular a venue it would become. It had raked seating at one end, and above it a gallery with more raked seating, and the stage projected out into the auditorium slightly, giving the open, vaulted area an intimacy it might otherwise have lacked. She imagined the stage was flexible, and could be extended or contracted to suit the production, and she found herself itching to see the other parts of the building and what else he'd done.

However, there was no opportunity, at least not at the start. The function started like a cocktail party, with everyone talking over everyone else until Jemima thought her head would explode with the brilliant laughter and the witty repartee. She smiled until she thought her face would crack, and then at eight o'clock the opening ceremony started.

Sam was whisked away to the stage with all the relevant and irrelevant dignitaries, who spoke ponderously about the historical role of the Maltings in the local community, and the history of the buildings themselves, and the transformation that Sam and his team had achieved.

The chairman of the borough council talked then about Sam. 'We decided to put the contract out to international competition, because we felt it was important that we should achieve something significant here to take the borough through into the new millennium with a flagship community centre, and a competition seemed the best way.

'The response was overwhelming, and amongst the submissions was one from Sam Bradley. He was a young and relatively untried architect, a bit of an unknown quantity and somewhat of a gamble. We were impressed by his initial design submission, not only by the designs themselves but by the professional way they were executed and the sound foundation of surveying that had been the basis for his submission.

'His team won the contract against significant international competition, and, looking around you now, I'm sure you'll agree that our faith in him was justified. Indeed, he's succeeded beyond our wildest imaginings, and I'm going to tell you this because I know he won't—he heard tonight that he's won a Design Centre award for this project, and we're proud to have been associated with it. Congratulations, Sam. Ladies and gentlemen, I give you Sam Bradley.'

The crowd cheered and applauded, and Sam got to his feet and smiled confidently and waved them down, and only Jemima and maybe his parents knew how nervous he was.

He scanned the crowd and found her, and his eyes locked with hers for a second. So proud she thought she would burst, she willed her courage to him, and with an almost invisible wink he turned his attention back to the wider audience.

'You're very kind,' he said with a grin. 'It could have

gone so easily the other way. What we've tried to do here has been daring, and we didn't know if we'd be able to pull it off, but now, seeing it finished, I'm pretty sure we got it right. I wondered along the way if we'd come in on time, but the gods were obviously on our side, despite a few little demons that tried to upset the applecart.'

There was a ripple of laughter from the crowd, and he went on with a smile, 'The award is a real bonus, and I'm thrilled for the team that we've won it. They've all worked so hard—everybody has—and I'd just like to thank all of those involved who've put in so much effort to make this the opening of something I hope everyone in the borough will enjoy and use for a long time to come. That was the idea—I hope it comes to pass, and I'm just grateful that I was given the opportunity to do it for you. Thank you for your faith in me.'

He sat down to thunderous applause, and after a moment the chairman of the borough council stood up and led the party off the stage. The ceremony concluded with the unveiling of a plaque set on the wall of the theatre building, and then he announced that a buffet supper was served in the restaurant next door, and that there was an exhibition of the progress of the restoration in the art gallery upstairs.

Jemima stood in the laughing, chattering crowd, feeling alone and separate, and waited for Sam to come and find her.

It took ages. He was mugged by everyone, all the glittering women with sparkling jewels and sinuous bodies and portly and successful husbands, and the clever people with designer evening clothes and bright witty conversation—people from his world, people he knew, who knew him and wanted to know him, especially tonight.

He reached her side and introduced her to the trail of people still following him, and, taking her hand, he led her through towards the restaurant.

'Unless I'm sorely mistaken,' he grinned in a second of quiet, 'you're ravenous.'

She smiled sheepishly. 'How did you guess?'

He laughed and squeezed her hand. 'Easy. Come on, let's find some food.'

But it wasn't that simple. They were intercepted at every step, and she marvelled at the cheerful and friendly way he dealt with the sycophantic crowd while still proceeding towards the restaurant.

Finally they were there, and Jemima managed to clear her plate before Sam had been given a chance to take more than a couple of bites of the delicious morsels.

He eyed her empty plate, laughed and swapped over, and she finished his off while he talked to yet another potential client.

'You ought to come and see it—it's lovely, but it needs a real master to restore it properly,' a woman was saying, purring up at him.

Jemima wanted to scratch her eyes out, but Sam just laughed and said she was too kind and dished out yet another card and told her to contact him.

There was a lull, and he grabbed a satay stick off the plate and lifted it to his mouth just as someone came up and slapped him on the back. It prodded his lip, and he sighed and put it down and turned round, laughing and talking again, while Jemima tried to find something safe for him to eat.

Finally, though, even Sam's patience came to an end.

'We'll eat later—come on, I want to show you the exhibition.'

He towed her upstairs, dishing out cards to people who stopped him, and then talked her round the exhibition.

At least, he tried to, but it was hopeless. 'Come and look at it tomorrow morning when there's no one here,' he said with a groan, and took her back downstairs.

'Where are we going now?' she asked.

'Somewhere we can be alone.'

'The loo?' she suggested wryly, and he chuckled.

'The theatre—they've got a band on the stage and the lights will be low. I might be able to sneak around undetected for a while, and anyway it'll give me a chance to dance with you.'

'I didn't know you liked dancing.'

His eyes warmed. 'I like holding you, and I haven't had a chance.'

They slipped through the door and melted into the little crowd. The lights were low, and he drew her into his arms and sighed as they swayed together to the music. 'You look stunning tonight; did I tell you that?'

She glowed inside. 'You said something, but don't let that stop you saying it again.'

He chuckled, and touched her arm lightly. 'What's with the gloves?'

She gave a rueful smile. 'My hands—I didn't want everyone thinking I was one of the construction team.'

'Oh, Jem!' He laughed softly and hugged her, then rested his chin on her head and sighed again. 'Thank God it's over. I can relax.'

'You were wonderful,' she told him, tipping her head back and looking up into his eyes. 'I was so proud of you I thought I'd burst.'

'I was scared to death until I saw you. Then somehow it was all right, as if you'd transferred your calm, unflappable spirit to me—'

'Calm and unflappable?' she said with a laugh. 'I am not—'

'You can be. You didn't flap about the snow and the power cut.'

'It was too depressing to flap. I just wanted to crawl into a corner—anyway, I had you to help me, thanks to Mary.'

'So you did.' His eyes crinkled at the corners as he remembered, and she felt his hands tighten and ease her closer. 'Come here, you're too far away.'

He felt good, warm and hard and strong, his powerful legs shifting against hers as they swayed to the music, his back firm against her hands. She was so close to him her dress was going to have creases, but she didn't care. She was aroused, and so was he, and the rest of the crowd might not have existed. She wondered how long it would be before they could decently slip away and be alone. It would be wonderful to have him to herself—

'Sam! This is where you're hiding!'

He groaned softly into her hair and shifted away from her slightly, turning her so that she stood half in front of him. 'Don't move,' he growled out of the corner of his mouth, and anchored her in position with one firm hand on her hip.

Over her shoulder she was conscious of his brilliant social smile, the bright words, the diplomatic chatter that promised nothing and everything, and then the band started to play an unashamedly romantic number.

'Excuse us,' Sam said with a smile, and turned her into his arms. He took one hand in his, cradling it by her shoulder, the other hand resting lightly in the small of her back, and he whirled her away into the crowd.

He moved beautifully, utterly in tune with her, or maybe she was in tune with him. Whatever, they moved together as if they'd done it for years, and the heat started to build in her with every subtle shift of his body against hers. It was almost too much for her—and it was too much for Sam, as well.

'Let's get out of here,' he muttered, and they threaded their way through the crowd yet again, fielding attempts to engage them in conversation—until they bumped into his parents in the foyer.

'Ah, Sam, we wondered where you'd got to—any chance of a coffee and a bit of peace and quiet?' his father asked.

Jemima's heart sank. It was the last thing she'd imagined on the agenda, but there was no way he could turn them away.

Or was there?

'Sorry,' he said with a smile—a genuine one this time. 'Jemima's been up since four, I've had an average of three hours' sleep a night for the last week, and frankly we were going to crash. I'll come and see you tomorrow. I'm sorry.'

His parents looked from Sam to Jemima and back again, and slow smiles spread on their faces. 'That's all right, darling, you get an early night,' his mother said, altogether too understandingly, and Jemima felt colour rush up to the roots of her hair.

'We're very proud of you—you've done well,' his father said, pumping his hand and patting his shoulder, and his mother kissed him goodbye, pecked Jemima on her burning cheek and said something about meeting her again soon.

Then they were free, crossing the courtyard, slipping into the lobby, dodging a crowd coming down in the lift by nipping into the maintenance stairwell and running up the three flights to the top, then sneaking across the landing and into the flat.

Sam pushed the door to and leant back against it, pulling her into his arms and laughing. 'We did it!' he crowed. 'It's like bunking off school—I feel really wicked.'

She tapped his nose with her fingertip. 'You shouldn't have put your parents off.'

'Why? I didn't want them here. Jemima, I want to be alone with you.'

His eyes darkened, the smile fading, and his mouth came down and brushed hers, just lightly.

It was enough. Heat leapt between them, and he took her mouth hungrily, cradling her head with one hand while the other cupped her bottom and lifted her hard against him. 'I want you,' he murmured against her lips, and what little strength was left in her legs deserted her completely.

'Sam,' she whispered, almost incoherent with need, and he carried her through to the bedroom and set her down on the edge of the bed.

'How does this undo?' he asked, fingers trembling.

'Just the zip—I have to wriggle out of the neck bit.' She felt the zip slide down, and Sam grasped the hem and lifted it, easing it over her head.

Then he dropped it on the floor, and his jaw nearly joined it.

She smiled. 'The last time you saw this—'

'—it was tied to sticks in a snow drift,' he finished, and a strained smile touched his mouth. 'It looks better on you than it did on the sticks.'

She chuckled and looked down at the red bra and suspender belt. With the long black gloves, black lacy knickers and black stockings they looked wicked and exciting, and Sam's reaction was everything she could have hoped for.

'Just don't move,' he said tersely, and peeled off his clothes, throwing the immaculate dinner suit onto the white carpet without a care. Then he reached for her, and with a little cry of relief she went into his arms...

His suit was covered in white fluff from the wool carpet, and so was her dress. She picked them up, shook them out and draped them over a chair, then tugged on his shirt and her black lace knickers and went to put the kettle on. It was five-thirty, milking time, and her body clock had woken her as usual.

With nothing to do and Sam still asleep, she went upstairs to the sitting room and opened the doors to the balcony, breathing deeply. The air smelt stale, though, with a slightly bitter tang from the exhaust fumes, and she listened to the rumble of the traffic, the honking horns, the hooter of a train, the boats chugging on the Thames below her, and she felt incredibly homesick for her cows and chickens and the mistle thrush that sang outside her window every morning.

Sam was at home here in this world, but it was alien to her now, and she remembered how miserable she'd been when she'd lived in London. Shivering, she stepped back inside and closed the doors, then turned to find Sam watching her oddly from the top of the stairs.

'I missed you,' he said, his voice morning-gruff and sexy. 'I woke up and you weren't there.'

Like every other morning, she thought sadly. 'Milking

time,' she said by way of explanation, and hugged her arms round herself.

He frowned. 'You look freezing. Come back to bed—I've made some tea.'

She went, smiling brightly to disguise her unhappiness, and he tucked her up in the bed against a great heap of pillows, climbed in beside her and handed her a mug of tea.

Then he leant over and kissed her softly on the mouth. 'Good morning.'

Is it? she wanted to say. She didn't. She just smiled and sipped her tea and sighed softly. 'I needed that,' she said, handing him the mug. 'Any chance of another one?'

'In a minute.' He put the mugs down and drew her into his arms again, cradling her against his shoulder. 'Thanks for being there for me last night. I really was dreading it.'

'You're welcome.'

His fingertip stroked her arm, tracing the words 'Won Award' that she'd written on it last night, and she shifted in his arms so she could see him. 'Did I tell you how proud I am of you?' she murmured.

'You said something, but don't let that stop you saying it again,' he said with a smile, echoing her words of the night before.

She smiled and cupped his cheek, loving the feel of the stubble against her palm. She was going to miss him when she went back—

'Jemima, I love you,' he said suddenly, and her hand froze against his jaw. 'Actually, I think I've loved you since you were six.' His jaw worked slightly, and he gave a self-conscious laugh and turned his head so his lips were soft against her palm. His hand came up and took hers, cradling it, and he shifted so they were lying face to face. 'I know I love you now, like I've never loved anyone. It's never felt like this—as if I daren't let you go because you're the most important thing that's ever happened to me in my life.'

'Oh, Sam,' she whispered, and her eyes filled with tears. 'I love you, too.'

'Marry me, Jem?' he murmured. 'Stay with me for ever. I need you so much.'

The tears spilled over and splashed on their hands, and a huge pain welled inside her. 'Oh, Sam, how can I? I've got the cows—'

'Owen wants them. You could sell them to him.'

'It's more than that—Sam, I got away from London because I hated it, and this weekend has just reminded me how much. I don't belong here—'

'We could move—we don't have to live here if you don't like it—'

'I do! I love the flat—all of this complex. I think it's wonderful, and I think you should be really proud of what you've achieved. It isn't that. It's—it's the people. All the bright and beautiful people, all chasing some unattainable dream—Sam, I hate it. It's so false. There's nobody here like Owen or your grandparents—people you can depend on in a crisis. The people you mix with are all too busy chasing their own dreams to have time for anyone else.'

'I think that's a little harsh,' he said quietly. 'I have a lot of friends I can depend on.'

'So do I—but they aren't here, Sam, and they never will be.'

His fingers traced her jaw, trembling, and his eyes were sad and a little lost. 'Jemima, I love you.'

'I love you, too, Sam, but it isn't enough.'

'It should be—'

'It isn't. I know it isn't. You forget, I spent years working in matrimonial law with people who couldn't live together even though they loved each other. And in the end, the love's destroyed. I'm sorry, Sam, I can't. I can't marry you and live here—I wouldn't be me, and after a while you wouldn't want me. I couldn't bear that.'

'I'll always want you.' His eyes closed and he pulled her into his arms and crushed her against him. 'Think about it,' he said, and he sounded choked. 'Think about it and let me know. Don't rush.'

'I don't need to rush—'

'Shh. Not now. Let me love you.' His hands slid under the shirt and cupped her breasts, and his mouth found hers with desperate urgency.

Jemima's heart ached. Whatever he might say it was the last time, their swansong, and she could hardly bear it. Their lovemaking was bittersweet, almost silent except for their muffled cries, and at the end she wasn't sure if the tears on her cheeks were Sam's or her own…

He drove her home later that morning, again almost in silence. There was nothing to say except the words neither of them wanted to hear, and so they didn't talk. Instead he held her hand, cradled against his thigh, and she fought back the tears and tried not to think about losing him.

When at last he pulled into the farmyard and refused a cup of tea she was almost glad, because she couldn't bear to prolong the goodbye. He saw her to the door, put her case inside and then met her eyes.

'Don't say anything,' he murmured unsteadily. 'Just

think about what I said. We wouldn't have to live there—there are other places.'

She shook her head numbly. 'I can't go back to London, Sam. I'm sorry. You'll never know how sorry, but I can't.' She touched his cheek with her roughened hand, and it just seemed to point up all their differences.

'I love you,' she told him, and forced herself to meet his eyes. They seemed to flinch at her words, but he didn't look away.

'Just not enough,' he finished.

'Our worlds are just too far apart now, and I can't go back. I've made the great escape, and I'm a different person. That doesn't mean I don't love you, or think you're wonderful, because I do.' Her eyes filled and flooded over, and with a gruff cry he pulled her into his arms and crushed her against his chest.

'Jem, don't,' he whispered raggedly. He let her go, stepping back and striding away, then he turned and came back, taking her mouth in a kiss so desperate it was almost savage.

Then he turned on his heel and went back down the path almost at a run.

'Goodbye, Sam,' she called, but her words were lost in the roar of the engine and the scrunch of tyres as he whipped out into the lane and sped off.

She sagged against the doorpost, her legs like jelly, and listened to the fading sound of his car. It drifted away to nothing, and then came the steady, rhythmic crunching of heavy footfalls on the path.

She blinked and focused on a dear, familiar face, and then it swam again, blurring into the background.

'Oh, dear. Like that, is it?' Owen said softly, and she fell into his arms and cried until she thought her heart would break.

* * *

Sam drove aimlessly for a while, then turned back. He wasn't sure what he was doing, but somehow he found himself on his grandparents' drive. His grandmother came out, dusting flour off her hands, took one look at him and wheeled him into the kitchen by the Aga.

'We won the award,' he told her expressionlessly.

'I know—your mother rang. Congratulations—but that wasn't what you came to tell me.'

'No.' Misery settled over him like a soggy blanket, and he slumped into a chair and leant his head against the wall, closing his eyes. 'I've done something rather stupid.'

She put the kettle on. He could hear her, clattering around, running taps and opening the tea caddy—comforting, familiar sounds that soothed him.

She slid a cup of tea across the table to him, and he opened his eyes and leant over it, chasing a bubble round the top with a fingertip. 'I asked Jemima to marry me.'

She said nothing, just waited, and he felt a huge lump rise up and threaten to choke him.

'She said no,' he got out past the lump, and squeezed his eyes shut. He had this insane, overwhelming urge to crawl onto her lap and cry his eyes out, and he pressed his fingers into his eyes and struggled to control his breathing. When it was a little steadier he opened his eyes and found his grandmother looking at him with sympathy.

'Don't be nice to me, for God's sake,' he said gruffly.

'All right, I won't. I take it the problem is where you both work?'

He nodded.

'And she won't move to London, of course. She hated it. She was miserable when she arrived here, but she was still happier with her cows and chickens than she had been in the city.'

He nodded miserably.

'So what are you going to do about it?'

He shrugged. 'Go back to London and try and forget about her, I suppose,' he said with commendable calm.

'Before or after you let go of that pain that's eating a hole in you?'

His chest heaved, and the next thing he knew his face was buried in a warm, soft bosom, a kindly hand was cradling the back of his head, and he was howling his eyes out like a baby.

The weeks dragged by. Jemima felt exhausted, pulled down by the weather and the pain of saying goodbye to Sam, and so she turned the cows out early and let them churn up the still-soft pasture. It was stupid, and she'd probably regret it later, but just now she was too tired to muck out and too poor to get the tractor fixed.

With that in mind, she went to Dorchester on the bus, taking the little black dress back to the nearly-new shop, and was paid for one of her suits that had sold.

Feeling rich, she went into a little coffee shop and bought a coffee and a Danish pastry, and had to leave them and run outside, suddenly queasy. She went to a park, sat down and stared at her cracked and work-worn hands, waggling her fingers and counting weeks.

Five—well, five and a half weeks since she'd fallen in the river, three weeks since she'd seen him last. Probably seven weeks since her last period.

No wonder she was tired.

She went to a chemist, bought a pregnancy test kit and took it home. She looked at it for two hours before she could bring herself to do the test, and when the little strip turned blue her heart thumped.

She was pregnant. Sam's baby was growing inside her, and in seven months or so she would be a mother. 'A baby, Noodle. What do you think of that?' she said to the dog, and she wagged her curly little tail and grinned.

Jemima sat down on the kitchen chair with a thump, and stared at the strip. She'd brought it downstairs from the bathroom with her and couldn't bring herself to throw it out, just in case. In case of what, she didn't even consider.

Jess, lying outside on the step, growled menacingly and began to bark, and Jemima stuffed the little strip into the kitchen bin hastily.

'Hello, Owen,' she called through the door, and her neighbour came in, Jess growling at his heels, and nodded to her.

'You all right?' he asked gruffly.

'I think so. How's your arm?'

He waggled it, newly out of plaster, and winced. 'Bit on the tender side. Been overdoing it, of course. See you've put the beasts out.'

She nodded. 'Yes. They were—um—getting a bit much, without the tractor to do the mucking out.'

He put the kettle on and sat himself down opposite her, fiddling with a box lying on the table. 'Don't suppose you want to sell them to me as a wedding present?'

'No, I don't—a what? Owen, you dark horse! Congratulations!' She leapt up and went round to hug him, and Jess growled threateningly from her position by the Rayburn. 'Jess, shut up, he's not getting married to me.'

The dog subsided, and Owen, once he'd finished

blushing, told Jem all about it. 'Seems she's had a soft spot for me for ages, but didn't like to say so. When I asked her out and she said no, she was just playing it cool, expecting I'd ask her again.'

'Except that you didn't.'

'No—not for nearly a year. Stupid, isn't it? Still, I'd spent a lot of time in there, chatting to her over the bar, so I suppose we got to know each other a bit like that.'

'And now you've asked her to marry you and she's said yes?'

He nodded. 'I love her,' he confessed, looking a little uncomfortable with this admission of rank sentiment, and his eyes fell on the box he'd been playing with.

Jemima, blushing furiously, snatched it out of his way but not before he'd registered what it was.

'Jem?' he murmured.

'Don't you tell a soul,' she threatened, wagging a finger at him.

'Sam?'

'Of course Sam!' she exclaimed, scandalised. 'Who else?'

He shrugged. 'I don't know. You city types do things different.'

'I am not a city type,' she said firmly.

'No? Sorry. I could have sworn you were, with that fancy car you turned up in first of all—'

'That was then. This is now—and now I'm not a city type. I don't know if I ever really was.' She made them tea and sat down, and Owen stirred enough sugar into it to turn it to syrup and regarded her steadily.

'So, what are you going to do about it?' he asked.

'The baby? Have it, of course.'

'And carry on here?'

'Yes—well, I don't know,' she added, trailing to a

halt. 'Oh, Owen, I don't suppose I'll be able to, will I? The thing is, without the herd I can't afford the mortgage I had to take out to pay Uncle Tom's debts, and if I'm going back to work what would I want with all this lot?'

She gestured towards the window, and beyond it the farmyard, the cows, the hens, the pasture, the woodland—all of it needing maintenance, and that meant money. 'I suppose I'll have to go back to work.'

'As a solicitor?'

She nodded. 'Yes. I hated it—well, dealing with divorces, anyway. I suppose I could do another branch of law—conveyancing or something.'

'You wouldn't reconsider marrying Sam?'

She shook her head. 'Not if it means marrying half of London. Owen, you should have seen them all. You'd think they owned him, and he can deal with it. I can't.'

'Would you have to?'

She shrugged. 'The flat's open-plan and beautiful. That's where he works. There's no way a baby would fit in there. It would distract him, and there would be sticky fingermarks on the plate glass and the suede furniture, and it would fall down the stairs and brain itself—no, it wouldn't work.'

She sipped her tea and looked across the mug at Owen. 'I don't suppose you'd like to buy a herd of cows as a wedding present for Jenny?'

CHAPTER TEN

SAM was busy.

He was busier than he'd ever been in his life, even at the end of the Maltings project, and that suited him down to the ground. He didn't like being alone in the flat with nothing to do, because every time he stood at the balcony doors he thought of Jemima. Every time he sat on the settee he thought of Jemima. Every time he lay down alone in his bed he thought of Jemima.

He didn't know missing someone could cause such disruption, could bleed all the colour from a glorious day, could take all the laughter out of even the funniest film.

Music killed him—the songs they'd danced to, all the bittersweet love songs that seemed to be playing in every shop he went into. Even his classical music was a no-go area, and he'd taken to listening to Radio 4 in the car.

He seemed to be spending his life in the car. The project that had followed the Maltings was under way, didn't seem to need much of his attention and left time for following up all the enquiries he'd had after the award had become his.

Oddly enough, several of them were south-west of London—Surrey, Hampshire, Wiltshire—even one in Dorset, although not as far west as Jemima. So he drove, and he lunched with clients, and he drove on again for dinner with other clients, and inevitably someone would ask about Jemima.

'We aren't seeing each other any more,' he'd explain, and stifle the pain the words caused.

His parents were harder to deal with, because they worried about him constantly and said he looked awful.

He did look awful. He'd taken to avoiding the mirror except in emergencies, and even then he couldn't meet his own eyes. There was something too wounded, too deep to deal with lurking in their sunken depths, and so he didn't look and carried on working as long as they would stay open, and then fell into bed and tried not to think of the soft warmth of Jemima's body snuggled up against him, or the gentle touch of her hands, or the incredible tenderness of her embrace.

Then one day, about five weeks after the opening, he had a phone call from one of his clients.

'Sam? Darling, it's Moya. I need you to come over and go through these plans with me again—we've changed our minds about the roof garden, and we thought—well, look, could you come over? It's awfully hard to explain.'

His heart sank. Moya Kennedy was a difficult woman, terminally indecisive and spoilt to death. 'Sure, Moya,' he agreed without enthusiasm. 'When?'

'Today?'

He looked at his schedule. He had a client in London at eleven, then another at three. He'd planned to get his hair cut and go for a walk around another site he was tendering for in between, but—

'How about twelve-thirty, quarter to one?'

'Lovely—I'll give you lunch. You're a darling.'

He didn't feel like a darling. He went to his first client, had difficulty parking and narrowly escaped a fine. He didn't want the job, anyway. He didn't agree with the client about what was right for the house, and so he declined the opportunity to design the alterations. The client then took the hump and got very sniffy about it, and he left knowing he'd burned his boats with a large section of the Hampstead community.

Oh, well, tough. He was busy enough anyway. He headed for Moya's house, parked in the road outside on a double yellow line and went in. He'd stick the parking fine on her bill, he decided.

'Sam, darling, do come in.'

He did a mild double take. Moya was dressed—if that was the word—in a very skimpy little negligee over not a lot, he suspected, and her sunbed goggles were perched in her expensively streaked hair. There was the odd strand of grey in it now, he noticed—probably more, under the streaks. He went past her into the hall, and, gathering up a tray of nibbles, she ushered him up to the top floor where they were planning a roof garden off their bedroom.

'I'll bring this up with us and we can eat while we look at the plans—to save time.'

'Good idea,' Sam agreed, following her to the top of the house. 'I'm a bit pushed today. So, what was the problem?'

'Oh, we've got a few changes we wanted to make—we thought a conservatory might be nice over part of it, but then we thought—well, look, here are the designs. Rob's scribbled a few notes for you, but he's had to go away and he's left me all alone. You look at them while I get something on—you caught naughty me on the sunbed, napping. Back in a tick. Have a nibble.'

She set the tray down on the bed, patted his arm and disappeared into the bathroom.

He scanned the notes scattered on the bed, sitting down on the edge while he ran his eye over the changes.

There was nothing major, really—nothing that couldn't have come to him in the post and been dealt with quite easily. He began to feel a prickle of irritation, and then Moya came out of the bathroom dressed in even less than before, and he closed his eyes.

'Moya—'

'Sam, come on, relax, live a little. Rob's away; we're safe.' Her fingers tugged at his tie, sliding the knot, and Sam caught her hand and stilled it.

'No, Moya,' he said softly, and stood up, his eyes still closed. 'This isn't right. It's not what I want. Don't go and spoil our relationship. We've worked together for years now—don't throw it all away.'

'Throw it away? Sam, why do you think we've had all the work done? Why do you think I keep getting you back? Sam, I love you!' She tucked her arm in his, sliding against him, her other hand on his chest, plucking at the fabric. 'Rob's no good for me any more—he can't—well, you know.' Her hand slid lower. 'Sam, please, I need you.'

He felt suddenly terribly sorry for Rob who couldn't, and for Moya, who wanted to. He lifted his lids and stared into Moya's dewy cornflower-blue eyes, and wondered if they were coloured contacts.

Probably.

He arrested her hand before it went any lower. 'Moya, I'm sorry, this isn't going to work.'

'What's wrong with me? Look at me, Sam—what's wrong with me?'

She turned slowly round, and he did look, and what he saw made him sad. She was ageing—slowly, and quite gracefully—but she fought against it every inch of the way. She was tanned all over, so bad for her but a fashion necessity, apparently, and, apart from the pert breasts that had benefited from enhancement, she was slim to the point of being thin.

He remembered someone telling him that women could never be too rich or too thin, and he disagreed. There was such a thing as being too thin, and Moya was too thin. By now she should have had soft curves and a mellow light in her eyes, not silicone implants and that frantic desperation he could see behind the contact lenses.

'Moya, I'm sorry,' he repeated, and, leaning over, he kissed her cheek, just once, gently.

'But what about the plans?' she wailed.

'Send them to me,' he told her. Then he turned on his heel, ran downstairs and let himself out, to find a traffic warden supervising the loading of his car onto a tow truck to remove it to the police pound.

'Look, I don't have time for this,' he told the woman. 'Let me give you a cheque for the fine and let me go.'

'Sorry, it can't be done. You have to go to the pound to collect it. The paperwork's all completed.'

He was tempted to tell her what to do with her paperwork, but it wouldn't have done any good. Instead he ground his teeth, hitched a lift with the driver of the recovery vehicle and paid his fine at the pound.

By the time he got it back he was late for his three o'clock client, and that lost him the job. There was also a message on his answer-phone from another client.

'Sam, it's Mike. I need a place in London to entertain. I don't suppose you know where I could get a flat like yours? Call me.'

He thought over his day, poured himself a hefty Scotch and rang Mike back. 'Sorry, I don't,' he told him. 'Only mine, and it's not for sale.'

'I'd pay you whatever you wanted.'

Sam laughed. 'Make me an offer.'

So he did, and Sam almost choked on his Scotch. 'I'll be in touch,' he told Mike, and cradled the phone. London was beginning to get on his nerves, and he wondered if perhaps Jemima wasn't right. If he sold the flat to Mike for the figure he'd talked about, he could buy a place down in Dorset near Jemima, convert part of it into a studio and work from home down there.

And Jemima wouldn't have to live in London, or leave her precious herd, and then maybe, when they'd had time to get to know each other better, perhaps then she'd marry him.

Her farm would be ideal, of course, only the cows needed the buildings and the house wasn't big enough to provide studio space for him. Besides, clients couldn't be expected to come and clamber over the muckspreader to get to the front door, and for all he knew Jem wouldn't want it anyway.

He finished his Scotch, did some paperwork that had been hanging over him and went to bed, then in the morning he contacted several estate agents in Dorchester and asked them to send him details of anything they had for sale in her area.

He had to go to Kent immediately afterwards, to see a client about the conversion of an oast house, and after he'd gone into considerable detail, they agreed he should go and draw up some preliminary sketches.

He had another call on the way home, and he didn't get back before late, so he had a take-away delivered, ate it at the drawing board and fell into bed after midnight.

The post arrived the following morning just before he went out, and there were several envelopes from Dorchester. He glanced at his watch, slit them open quickly and then sat down on the bottom step with a bump.

'Puddleduck Farm?'

He scanned the details, his mind racing, and picked up the phone, jabbing in his grandmother's number. She answered on the second ring, and he didn't give her time to get the number out.

'Grannie, what the hell's Jemima up to?' he growled.

'Ah. I was going to ring you today. Um—I don't really know how to tell you this.'

'Just spit it out. What's she doing?'

'She's put the farm on the market—and she's letting Owen have her uncle's prize herd as a wedding present.'

'What?' Sam felt the shock drain all the blood from his face, and his heart felt cold. 'Owen—Owen Stockdale?' he roared.

'Perhaps you'd better come down and talk to her, if you still care. She doesn't look well.'

'I don't look well, either. Damn it, Grannie, why the hell didn't you tell me sooner?'

'I only just found out—and don't swear at me, Sam.'

'Sorry.'

'So, are you coming down?'

'Too damn right.'

'Good.' She sounded satisfied, and Sam could have strangled her. 'I'll make the bed up for you. Will you be down today?'

Sam thought of all the appointments he had, and the pressure of work piling up, and gave a harsh sigh. 'Yes. I'll see you later.'

He banged the phone down, threw a few things into a case and ran down to the car. He made Dorset in less than two hours, ignoring most of the speed limits, and pulled onto Jemima's drive at ten o'clock, just as she was turning the cows out.

'Sam!' she said, and she felt the colour wash out of her cheeks.

'I want to talk to you,' he said tightly, and, grabbing her arm, he ushered her into the kitchen. Noodle and Jess mugged him, and he patted them absently while Jemima rubbed her arm and glared at him.

'Don't manhandle me, Sam. I don't like it.'

'Sorry.' He slapped the house details down on the kitchen table under her nose, and she gave a quiet sigh. This wasn't quite what she'd expected, but she supposed they had to start somewhere—

'What the hell is this all about?' he asked tightly. 'My grandmother tells me you're marrying Owen Stockdale and giving him your uncle's precious herd, and then on top of that I get the details of your farm through the post from an estate agent!'

Jemima stared at him, sifting through all the erroneous information he was coming out with, and one thing emerged. He'd got the details of her farm from an agent—but why?

Because he was thinking of moving down here?

Hope blossomed in her chest, and she settled back against the sink, folded her arms and waited for the scene to play itself out.

'Owen's been very good to me,' she began.

'Hah!' Sam snorted. 'Good to you, my eye. He's only interested in your herd and your body—what about your mind, Jemima?'

'What about my mind? When did you take an interest in my mind, Sam?' she asked angrily. 'I seem to remember you were quite happy with my body—'

'At least I know what to do with it. What's he like in the sack, Jemima? Does he make your blood sing in your veins? Does the earth move for you when he makes love to you—or is that just his telescopic ram?' he spat disgustedly.

She giggled. She couldn't help it, it was only the tiniest sound, but Sam went mad.

'Dammit, Jemima!' he roared. 'Don't laugh at me—not any more! I know I've given you plenty to laugh at in the past, but this time I'm serious. There's no way I'm going to stand back and let you marry that ox of a man without a fight—even if he does know one end of a cow from the other. I mean, let's face it, there's no way Owen the Ox would get caught by the wrong end of a cow, not like good old Sam, and he wouldn't fall off the barn roof clearing the snow because he'd have some fancy bloody gadget to do it! Still, I can buy machinery. I can buy you a new tractor, and you can keep your herd that you love so much. I can do for you all the things Owen can do, and more, because I love you, Jemima, and he doesn't.'

She glanced at the table. 'So, why did you get the details of the farm, Sam?'

'Because like a fool I thought I'd come down here and be near you, and then perhaps I could get you to change your mind.'

She looked down at her hands, cracked and sore, but not for much longer, hopefully.

'I won't change my mind,' she told him gently. 'I can't live in London—'

'So why marry Owen? Just to spite me?'

'Do you really think I'd do that?'

He gave a sharp sigh and stabbed his hands through

his hair. 'I don't know. I'm beginning to think I don't know you as well as I thought I did.'

She decided to put him out of his misery. 'I'm not marrying Owen, Sam.'

He lifted his head slowly and met her eyes, his own confused. 'What?'

'I'm not marrying Owen.'

'But—my grandmother said you were letting him have the cows as a wedding present.'

'I am, sort of. He's marrying Jenny.'

Comprehension dawned, and his eyes narrowed. 'Did my grandmother know that?'

'I expect so.'

'And yet she let me think—damn her!'

He turned, staring out over the valley, his jaw working furiously. 'OK, so you're not marrying Owen. So, why are you giving him the cows? I was under the impression you loved those cows, and yet you're giving them to that man without a backward glance—'

'Not without a backward glance,' she corrected. 'I'll miss them.'

'What—even Daisy?'

She smiled. 'Even Daisy.'

'But why, Jem? They're your pride and joy.'

She shook her head. 'They were Uncle Tom's pride and joy, and they were a way of staying here after he died, but—well, it's too hard now.' She chewed her lip, and her hands slid down and linked together over her baby. Sam's baby. Their baby.

'I'm pregnant,' she told him, and his head snapped round, eyes scanning her like lasers.

'What?' he breathed.

'I'm having a baby. That's why I'm selling up—to move to Berkshire and be near you, so you can spend time with your child. I can't live in London, and no child of mine would be brought up in a flat overlooking a London dockyard, but I thought if we were near enough, maybe you could commute, or we could split our time—'

'It's my baby?'

She met his incredulous eyes and smiled. 'Of course. Whose did you suppose it was?'

He shrugged and swallowed. 'Owen's?'

She laughed and shook her head. 'Jenny would kill me before she'd let me that close—and anyway, I've told you, Owen does nothing for me.'

Sam's mouth twitched slightly. 'Not even with his telescopic ram?'

She chuckled. 'Not even with that.' Her smile faded. 'I love you, Sam. I want to be near you, but it's important to me to be the woman I am, not the woman I'd be if we were in London—'

'Forget London. I hate it, too. I had my car impounded the day before yesterday, and it cost a fortune to get it back.' He held out his hand to her, and she reached out and took it. 'Marry me, Jemima. Let's live here with our baby, and we can do up the house and convert the buildings into a studio, and I can work from home.'

She looked round. 'But it's awful, Sam! You wouldn't want to live here! You've got a beautiful flat—'

'Mmm. Someone just made me an offer I can't refuse.'

'You'd sell it?' she said, shocked, and he nodded.

'Of course. Why not?'

'Because—I don't know! It's your baby—'

'No.' He laid a hand gently over the little curve in the cradle of her pelvis. 'This is my baby. That's just bricks and mortar. This is what matters.'

Her eyes filled, and with a little cry she threw herself into his arms. 'I thought you'd never leave it,' she sobbed, relief taking away the backbone that had supported her through the last few weeks.

'Silly girl. I said I would.'

'But—I never thought you were serious. I never thought you'd leave London. What about all your clients?'

He shrugged. 'What about them? More and more of them are in the country now, many of them between here and London. It's ideal to be here, because it means we don't have to fight with the London traffic to have meetings.'

'But you still wouldn't want to live here,' she said, looking round at the dingy little kitchen.

'It's delightful.'

'It's a mess.'

He grinned. 'It needs a little attention. You wait and see, it'll be lovely—and you'll have time to enjoy it. There'll be roses round the door—'

'There are roses round the door,' she pointed out, and he laughed.

'There you go, then. It's already perfect. What more could we want?'

She chewed her lip. 'I need to pay off my mortgage.'

He shrugged. 'So? I'll buy the farm off you anyway. It's your inheritance. You can put the money in a safe place and keep it, just in case you decide you get sick of me.'

'Or you get sick of me?' she said, dreading it.

'No. I'll never get sick of you,' he vowed, and drew her back into his arms. 'I've missed you, Jem,' he said, and his voice sounded suspiciously uneven. 'Life without you's been hell. I thought I'd be all right if I kept busy, but I wasn't. You were all I could think about, day and night—'

He broke off and squeezed her, and she slid her arms round his waist and hugged him back. 'Me, too. I was miserable. I didn't realise it was possible to miss anyone so much.'

'We should have talked to each other. You should have told me you were pregnant.'

'And have you insist I should marry you and go up there just because of the baby? I thought you'd move to Chelsea or Ealing or Richmond or somewhere like that and think it would be far enough—or alternatively you'd move down here and wreck your career—'

'I don't think you need to worry about my career. Since the award I've been turning away all the jobs that didn't interest me. I've made a few enemies—spoilt clients that wanted things I couldn't give.'

She tipped her head back. 'Sounds ominous.'

He laughed. 'There's a woman called Moya Kennedy. She—' His face twisted slightly. 'She propositioned me the other day.'

Jemima straightened in his arms. 'I hope you walked away.'

'Of course I did. I felt sorry for her—and her husband. She told me he can't any more.'

'Can't what—? Oh. Oh, poor man.'

'Quite. Anyway, seems all the work I've done for them over the years was because she fancied she was in love with me. I must be particularly dense, but it never even occurred to me.'

His arms cradled her against his chest, and he swayed slightly, rocking her. 'I love you, Jemima. There'll never be anybody else for me. You don't need to worry about my clients.'

'I'm not.' She eased away and looked up into his eyes. 'I trust you, Sam. I hope you trust me, too.'

He smiled wearily. 'Oh, I trust you. I'm not sure about Owen, but I trust you.'

She laughed. 'Owen's fine. Anyway, Jenny'll keep him busy for a few years.'

'Good.' Sam moved away from her. 'Mind if I use your phone?'

She hid a smile. 'Don't tell me—your grandmother?'

He just grinned. 'How did you guess?'

She put the kettle on while he rang her, then turned to see him lounging in the doorway, watching her hungrily.

'Don't suppose you need a nap, do you, after your drive?' she suggested with a little smile, and his mouth tipped into a crooked, sexy grin.

'You read my mind.'

She pulled the kettle off the hob, held out her hand and led him up the stairs…

It was a simple and beautiful wedding, in the new register office at the Maltings. They'd decided on London because all their various families and friends were near there, with the exception of Owen and Jenny and Sam's grandparents, who'd travelled up for the day together in Owen's father's car.

Owen's parents were going to look after all the dogs, and the cows were now officially Owen's anyway. Jemima was relieved. She'd found it difficult, and since they'd gone she'd done nothing but sleep.

It had taken two weeks to arrange the wedding, but Sam wouldn't give her any longer. 'I've had enough scares,' he'd said. 'The sooner we tie the knot, the better—and anyway, Mike wants the flat.'

He'd sold it to his friend complete with all the furniture, because it would have looked daft in a country cottage, and he'd put almost all his other things in store ready for the move. The tools of his trade were installed in a rented studio space in Dorchester, until the conversion was ready, and apart from their overnight things and a few personal bits and pieces the flat was ready to hand over on the Monday.

They were married on a late April Saturday, with sunshine sparkling off the Thames and flashing on the wings of the gulls, and Jemima thought it was fitting that the turning point in their lives should be recorded in the place that had been the turning point in Sam's career.

The reception was held in the restaurant, with the doors open to the riverside, and after all the speeches the tables were cleared and a DJ set up his gear and played nothing but love songs.

There were oldies, wonderful songs like 'Crazy' by Patsy Cline, and classics like 'The First Time Ever I Saw Your Face' by Roberta Flack, but all unashamedly romantic and absolutely perfect for dancing.

And they did dance. Sam smiled at all the people that wanted to talk to them, took Jemima in his arms and whisked her onto the dance floor, ignoring them all.

Some of the numbers were slow, others faster, and as the time went by they grew more daring, until in the end they were jiving, with Sam throwing her around at the end of his arm and everyone clapping and cheering them on.

Finally they had to stop, exhausted and laughing and exhilarated to find that they were so closely in tune.

'You are one slick mover, Mr Bradley,' Jemima said, falling into a chair and chuckling.

'You're pretty smooth yourself, Mrs Bradley.'

'I might have known you'd be a good dancer,' she said with a wicked twinkle, and to her delight he coloured slightly.

'I don't know what you mean,' he murmured, but he was smiling, and she chuckled and patted his cheek.

'Later,' she promised.

A shadow fell across them, and she looked up to see Owen there. 'I can't compete with that—Jenny tells me I've got two left feet—but I wonder if you could spare your wife for just one dance?'

Sam met his old rival's eyes and smiled slowly. 'I should think so—on one condition. You return the favour.'

Owen nodded, and Sam unfolded himself from his chair and crossed over to where Jenny was sitting. Jemima looked up into Owen's eyes, and let him draw her to her feet.

'You look beautiful,' he told her gruffly, and he wrapped her hand in his, laid the other lightly against her spine and held her at a careful distance while he swayed with her to the music. 'I hope you're happy, Jem,' he murmured. 'You deserve to be.'

'I am—I hope you and Jenny will be—you deserve it, too.'

'You'll come to the wedding in June?'

'Of course.'

'Won't be fancy like this.'

She smiled. 'Owen, weddings aren't about being fancy. They're about two people who love each other starting the rest of their lives together. That's why it's important to have friends there—to share in it. We'll be at your wedding, just as you've been at ours. You can be sure of it.'

The music stopped, and Sam and Jenny appeared beside them. Owen released her to Sam, and gathered Jenny into his arms with obvious affection.

'I suppose we ought to go, so people can start getting away,' Sam said to her.

'Probably.'

They said goodbye to everyone, then headed for the door.

'Are you going to throw your bouquet to anyone?' Sam asked as they reached it.

She met his eyes. 'It's tradition—why?'

'Throw it to Jenny.'

'OK.' She smiled and turned, and with a flick of her wrist she sent the colourful posy arcing through the air towards Jenny and Owen.

She caught it with a little shriek of laughter, and waved happily, her eyes shining.

'He can't get out of it now,' Sam said, and, tucking her hand in his, he ran out of the door with her, through the hail of confetti and rice and well-wishers, and into the glass lobby. The lift was there, and they glided up to the top, opened the door of the flat and went in.

Then Sam turned to her and drew her into his arms.

'That was a fabulous day,' he murmured.

'Wasn't it? I'm glad we got married here.'

'Me, too. I'm glad we're spending the night here, too.'

'Why?'

'Because you don't have a jacuzzi.'

'Yet.'

He smiled slowly. 'Yet.'

'Better make the most of this one.'

'My sentiments entirely.'

He led her through into the bathroom, turned on the taps and came back to her. 'About this lovely dress—'

'Mmm?'

'How does it come off?'

She smiled. 'Easy.' She unzipped it, slid it down her arms and stepped out of the shimmering ivory puddle on the floor.

'And the rest.'

He peeled off his suit, never taking his eyes off her, then helped her into the bath and sat down at the other end, his toes sliding under her bottom and tickling her.

He pressed the button for bubbles, reached over for the champagne conveniently placed within reach, and popped the cork, pouring two tall flutes and handing her one.

'Here's to us, Mrs Bradley—all three of us.'

She lifted her glass. 'Our very good health,' she said with a smile, and sipped. The bubbles tickled her nose, and the bubbles in the bath tickled her everywhere else. She laughed in delight, lay back against the end of the bath and let her toes go walking up his thigh.

His eyes widened, and he put his glass down and knelt up, drawing her up into his arms.

'I love you,' he murmured, and then he proved yet again just what an amazing mover he was…

EPILOGUE

IT WAS a glorious April day, and the sun was warm on their faces. Everyone was leaving now, after the official opening of the studio, and Sam stood with one arm round Jemima, shaking hands with friends and clients old and new as they left.

'I think it's the best thing that could have happened to you, darling, and I'm sure it'll be wonderful,' his grandmother said, hugging him, and he hugged her back, absurdly pleased by her approval.

'I like the barns, too,' she added, and winked and pinched his cheek. He smiled, used to her cock-eyed humour, and his eyes flicked to Jemima's, sharing the joke.

Not that it was a secret that his grandparents thought Jemima was the best thing that had ever happened to him. They'd told him so—and Jemima—on a regular basis over the last year.

The baby fidgeted in Jemima's arms, and he lifted her easily to his shoulder and patted her back. She settled back to sleep again without a murmur, and Jemima turned and smiled up at him.

She looked wonderful—radiant with health and happiness—and behind them the barns were everything he'd hoped for.

He had a new studio in the cow barn, with the old Lister engine polished up and gleaming in pride of place in one corner, and a row of windows looking out over the valley that he loved so much. The other barns were to be used for holiday cottages, to give Jemima an income and an interest, and the cottage itself—well, it was home at last, and they both loved it.

Owen and Jenny were the last to leave, coming up to them with their tiny baby almost lost in Owen's arms, and it was good to see them looking so well and so happy.

It was good to see them leave, as well, because Sam had something to show Jemima. They waved them off, and he ushered her across the newly flagged yard to the kitchen door.

'Tea?' she suggested, kicking off her shoes and padding over to the new Aga.

'Later. I've got a surprise for you. Let's put Tiddler to bed first.'

Jemima smiled slowly and turned towards him. 'Yes, we don't want any interruptions, do we?'

'Not that kind of surprise,' he said with a lazy grin. 'Come on.'

She followed him, her brows twitching together in a little puzzled frown, and they went into Amy's room and tucked her up in her cot. She went down without a murmur, and then Sam took Jemima by the hand and led her into their bedroom.

Ridiculously, he felt nervous. It was silly, but he'd never shown anything like this to anyone before, and he suddenly wondered if she'd like it.

'There,' he said diffidently, and pointed at the wall.

A picture hung on the wall over the chest of drawers, a pen and ink drawing full of minute detail. Jemima crossed the room and stood close to it, slowly taking in the detail, and then she started to laugh.

'It's us!' she said delightedly, recognising the barn.

'Oh, look, here you are falling over with the crank handle of the Lister in your hand—and look! That's when you stood too close to Daisy's tail! Oh, Sam, it's wonderful—oh, you're falling off the roof! And mucking out, and fetching the water, and milking—is that Bluebell kicking over the bucket?'

She turned to him, laughing, and hugged him. 'It's wonderful! Who did you find to draw it? It's so accurate, almost as if the artist had been there.'

Sam coloured slightly, and Jemima narrowed her eyes.

'Sam? Did you do it?'

He nodded, looking very uncertain, and Jemima flung her arms round him and hugged him. 'Oh, Sam, it's wonderful! I didn't know you could draw!'

'I am an architect,' he said drily, from the depths of her hug, and she laughed and released him, turning back to the picture.

'That's different. This is—well, it's fabulous—but you haven't put me falling in the water.'

His face lost its smile. 'No. I didn't need any reminders of that. I thought I'd lost you.'

'Instead you ended up with Amy as well.'

The bleak look faded from his eyes, and he smiled again. 'Yes—thank God. I can't believe everything's turned out the way it has. I have to pinch myself sometimes just to believe it's real.'

'Oh, it's real, Sam. We're here, and we're staying.'

He turned her into his arms, his eyes serious. 'I love you,' he said softly. 'Don't forget that. There've been times over the past year when I've been difficult to live with, a bit distracted with all the building work and things, and I might not have told you as often as I should have, but I do love you.'

She felt a lump in her throat. 'I know you do. I love

you, too—and you haven't been that difficult to live with.'

'I was when the Aga didn't fit.'

She laughed and cradled his jaw in her hand. 'Just a teeny bit.' She went up on tiptoe and kissed him softly, lingeringly. One finger traced his lower lip, dragging slightly over the firm fullness.

'Are you busy?' she murmured.

One brow arched. 'Not especially. Got anything in mind?'

Jemima smiled, and thought how lucky she was to have found him. 'Seems a shame to waste the baby's nap.'

Sam drew her into his arms. 'Mmm.' He kissed her lightly, then lifted his head and looked down into her eyes. 'Happy anniversary, Mrs Bradley,' he whispered, and then he kissed her…

HARLEQUIN
PRESENTS®

Harlequin®
Historical

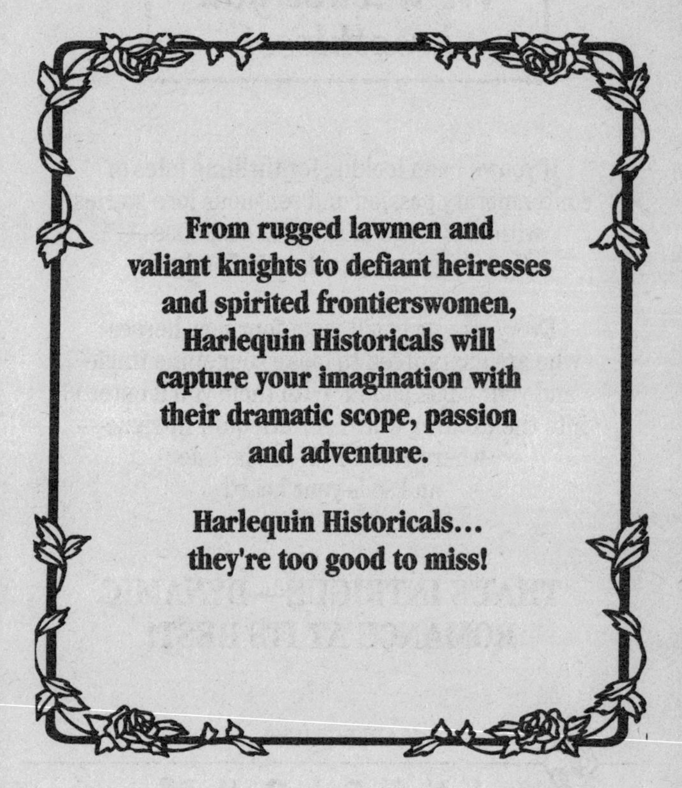

HARLEQUIN®
AMERICAN ROMANCE®